THE SILENT TREATMENT

BY

STEVE HALLOCK

For information, please address:
The Artists' Orchard, LLC
P.O. Box 113593
Pittsburgh, PA 15241

www.theartistsorchard.com

ISBN: 978-0-9964592-3-5

Produced in the United States of America

For Murray

In the attitude of silence the soul finds the path in a clearer light, and what is elusive and deceptive resolves itself into crystal clearness.

– Mahatma Gandhi

I

When words become unclear, I shall focus with photographs. When images become inadequate, I shall be content with silence.

– Ansel Adams

Her routine the night that Grant stopped talking was the same as every night. Pauline switched on the portable radio in the kitchen, poured herself a white wine and sat down to listen to the news on NPR.

The on-air reporter was reading from a New York Times story.

"After detaining him for weeks, the jihadists dragged him on Tuesday to a public square where a masked swordsman cut off his head in front of a crowd," the announcer read. "His blood-soaked body was then suspended with red twine by its wrists from a traffic light, his head resting on the ground between his feet, his glasses still on, according to a photo distributed on social media by Islamic State supporters."

The announcer then introduced the Times

reporter, who provided the details in an on-air interview. The dead man, the reporter said, had been the caretaker of archaeological artifacts for decades, exploring the ruins of his hometown, Palmyra, about 134 miles northeast of Damascus. He named his daughter after an ancient queen, Zenobia, "and he became so intertwined with its development," the reporter said in a soft, scrawling voice, "that one historian called him Mr. Palmyra. But his name, his friends would want you to know, was Khalid al-Assad."

"Enough." Pauline lifted her wine glass to her mouth and took a long sip, let it trickle down her throat and into her stomach, soothingly. The radio broadcast shifted into local headlines. The school board had approved the hiring of a new girls soccer coach, replacing the previous coach who had been found guilty of seducing the captain of the team. The state house was nearing a vote on the new fiscal budget. A local high school senior had died earlier that day after her car swerved off a rural county road and slammed into a tree. Police would not release her name and no other details were available, pending an investigation.

"Geesuz."

Another sip, then a gulp, of the calming

wine.

Pauline stood up, went into the darkened living room, then heard faint trumpet notes from the study. This is where she usually found Grant in the evening, sitting in his chair next to the table lamp with his own glass of wine – red, and dry – or on his knees searching through his shelves of his vinyl records collection for God knows what tonight – a nostalgic romp through the Beatles and Stones and Van Morrison and then on to the obscure rock groups of the '60s and '70s. Or it might be a blues night – Howlin' Wolf, Mayall, Clapton, Stevie Ray Vaughan. Or, the usual, jazz – a CD, a tape, some record yet unplayed from a collection he'd bought from a village library that was closing out its vinyl discs, to be replaced with CDs.

Another sip; Grant's jazz drifted into the living room, a slow piece. She recognized Miles Davis' breathy trumpet, and the tune; Grant had played it often and had told her the name of it. But she'd forgotten. Blues something.

Grant had told her that the library board members didn't know what they were giving up in parting with the albums, which included live jazz and classical performances over the last half of the 20th century, for 25 cents each – nearly $500 from his and Pauline's savings.

"I don't know about them, but we're giving up about 1 percent of your IRA," Pauline had said as Grant unloaded box after box of records from the van he'd borrowed from work.

Pauline shouted toward the study. "Hello!"

Nothing came back.

She turned on the living room light, and then the living room lamp next to the corner chair, as she continued her coming-home route toward the stairway that led from the front door to the bedrooms and bathroom upstairs. She poked her head into the study.

"Hello, I said." She smiled at Grant, who sat in his chair, his spectacles glistening from the dim lamp. She stood in the doorway, surrounded by Miles Davis trumpet notes, in her tan slacks, black pumps, pink blouse and blue sweater-vest.

Grant looked at her, didn't speak.

"Bad day, huh? I see there was a fatality today. You shoot it?" The living room light shone behind her, backlighting her face, creating a soft, yellow glow that ringed her head. "I'm going to make something to eat. You hungry?"

Grant did not answer.

Pauline went back to the kitchen, replenished her wine glass, took down a can of vegetable soup, opened it and spooned it into a sauce pan.

"Abby caught me in the parking lot and apologized," Pauline said into the study as she came back through the living room toward the stairs. "Said she doesn't usually get that drunk. Offered to pay to have my jacket cleaned."

She stopped at the doorway again. She glanced in at Grant, who sat fingering the rim of his wine glass, staring at the soft blue light of his stereo receiver; he hadn't touched his wine; the glass was full of deep red.

"I talked to Vicki today," she said as she started up the stairs. "Heather's over her cold, so Vicki went back to work. That's the sickest kid I've ever known. Colds, flu, colic, strep throat." Pauline's voice faded as she turned the corner of the stairway and went on up to their bedroom.

Her footsteps creaked on the old wooden floor above Grant. He heard the faint clanging of clothes hangers, saw her in his mind as she undressed, carefully hanging and folding the clothing of the day as she changed into sweats and socks. He heard the mattress and bed give as she sat down to take off her shoes and pull off her pantyhose, imagined her saying yet again, if he were up there with her, "God, I hate pantyhose, whoever invented it should be shot. It's like sitting in a glove all day, tight and hot."

So don't wear them, he'd told her.

And she'd looked at him, then sighed. "I want to look good for work. I don't want to be one of those women who get frumpy and don't care how they look at work."

But nobody can see them under the slacks, he would say.

"Yeah. But they help hold me in, y'know?"

He'd nodded.

Grant had always enjoyed being in the room when Pauline undressed. He liked watching her methodically peel away the articles of clothing. It was not sexy, the way she did it; but it made him feel comfortable, how she easily and casually took off her blouse and then her bra as he watched; he enjoyed seeing her breasts, still firm, before she slipped into the sports bra that was her leisure wear at home or that she wore to the gym when she went for an after-work session on the machines at the health club.

He liked it when they got ready for work together in the morning, and she undressed while he brushed his teeth. He always stopped and looked at her as she slipped out of her sleeping shirt and then her panties; she stood naked briefly for a moment while she reached into the shower, turned on the water and adjusted its temperature. Then she turned her back to him; he looked at the curvature of her body, the arc around her hips, as she carefully stepped into the shower and pulled the curtain shut.

Grant sat in the lamp glow of the stereo system's light and music and imagined Pauline upstairs going through all of her undressing and then dressing routine before coming back down to her dinner of soup, tossed salad and ice water. He leaned back and looked at the walls of his study, at the photographs he had taken during vacations with Pauline. The Tetons hung next to the opposite window, tall, cold, ragged, overlooking the valley in which lay the town of Jackson Hole. They'd stopped on a side road and Grant set up his tripod while Pauline peeled an orange and sucked on the fruit as Grant focused and adjusted and shot the Tetons, purple in the fading sunlight, their peaks a brilliant white as though topped with frozen whipped cream.

Grant had told Pauline that tetons was French for tits. Grand Tetons means big tits, he told her as she watched him put his camera gear away.

Pauline had grinned. "I knew that. That's probably the only reason you took that picture."

"Yeah, I can tell the guys at work that I spent my vacation shooting the biggest boobs I ever saw. I still prefer yours, though." He reached out and gently brushed his hand against Pauline's left breast, stopped and fingered it through her sweater.

"Not so grand," she said.

"Grand enough."

That night, they found a downtown cafe and ate dinner, then went to a nightclub that was in a basement of a corner building, where a rock band played '60s and '70s hits. Grant drank beers. Pauline sipped white wines; they always had to be white.

"I drank cheap red wine all through college," she'd said when Grant asked what it was she liked about white wines, even with spaghetti. "White wine somehow seems more mature, more sophisticated. I don't know. I guess I've gotten used to the taste."

Pauline drank more and talked less in those days, early in their marriage.

A photo of the Golden Gate Bridge hung next to the corner curio cabinet. The water was gray and choppy; the steel of the bridge sliced through a hazy sky. The white sail of a boat skimmed along the water, entering the shadow beneath the bridge. Grant had shot the photo from behind the railing of a boat they'd taken out on a group tour of the bay.

As the boat headed toward Alcatraz, Grant explained to Pauline that the waters were shark-infested. That's why the prisoners didn't escape.

"Which room do you suppose was Burt Lancaster's in 'The Birdman of Alcatraz?'" Pauline said, grinning at Grant.

They stood at the railing and watched the water, the ocean churning below them. The wind blew into the boat; it smelled fishy and salty. That night they went to North Beach and found a spaghetti house; Grant couldn't remember its name, but he could remember the dark wood inside, the smell of garlic and onion and vinegar dressing, the sharp taste of the red sauce in his mouth, which he washed down with a dry port. And then he and Pauline walked for blocks, listening to the neighborhood, watching their fellow tourists and the neighborhood residents on the sidewalks and streets, smelling the bread and flowers and old cement and stone of the neighborhood.

Grant and Pauline were people and neighborhood watchers.

A wide panorama of Pittsburgh glistened on the wall above the chair where Grant sat.

The glow of the skyscrapers filled the Mononga-hela River beneath the tall buildings like thousands of drops of wet light; the glass towers of the PPG building stood above the shimmering water, reflecting the neon and glare of the buildings around it, the headlights of the cars that filled the city streets. Grant shot the picture from Grand-view Avenue on Mount Washington, a residential ridge of apartments and condos and restaurants that looked out over the city. The view was of tiers of cement building blocks on frames of steel, roof-top gardens, trolleys and buses rolling in and out of downtown, blending with the automobiles to make squared tributaries of clean, white light all under a wide sky filled with stars and a broad haze of city light.

Pauline and Grant had eaten dinner around the family dining room table at Pauline's sister's house earlier that evening. Vicki was one of two siblings who had stayed behind in the family's home town. As the two families – Grant, Pauline and, their son, David, Vicki and her new husband, Dom – passed the tossed salad and grilled chicken and boiled potatoes around the table, Pauline and her sister talked at each other about their childhood, their parents, their siblings. Later, their laughter mixed with the television and the shouts of the neighborhood just beyond the front door screen as Grant sat on the front porch and listened to the noise, the soundtrack of his wife's life and family all around him.

On another wall, in the dining room, a blow-up Grand Canyon hung in a silver frame, its purple and pink rocks contrasting with a deep blue desert sky. Shadows and scrub foliage gathered in the crevices and layers of sedimentary rock of the sheer cliffs that climbed up out of the Colorado River that meandered, carrying the soaring rock with it, into the desert miles away. Twenty years ago, Grant and Pauline stood on the north rim of the canyon, higher by 1,000 feet than the distant south rim. They gazed down into the shadowy abyss, ventured a couple of steps closer to the edge of a cliff until a woozy stomach stopped Grant a couple of yards back. He peeked down as far as he could, saw the darkening lower canyon, the evergreen trees clutching to the sheer rock.

"This is fantastic," Pauline said. "I've seen movies of the Grand Canyon, but it seems bigger, deeper in real life."

They found a perch, took out their canteens and drank water, then Pauline pulled her legs under her so that she was sitting cross-legged Indian fashion, the sun shining onto her back, as Grant set up his tripod and camera and carefully took picture after picture, waiting for that moment like none other with the purples and pinks and blues and the slight hint of orange turning to pink as the sun set, when the colors are most vivid, the air so still – a moment of desert life mixing with the cool alpine community above it, with the birds chirping in the distance, the river a silent trickle far below, chipmunks and squirrels scampering in the underbrush. Pauline and Grant watched and listened to it all in silence, blessed silence, until a click of a camera filled the space around them like the clean cock of a gun hammer, only there was no blast following it. Just serenity.

Later, they sat on the stoop of their rental cabin. Grant had never seen stars as clear or as abundant, like millions of dots of gleaming dust, as those in the black Arizona sky above them.

Pauline's footsteps padded down the carpeted stairway. Miles Davis' trumpet floated through the room, hovered in the darkness, its tone mellow and golden like a bell ringing clearly in the still air. Pauline had changed into sweat pants and sweat shirt and a pair of sneakers. Her black hair – the thin streaks of gray couldn't be seen in the dimly lit room – stopped just below her ears. Her skin was pale, her cheekbones still high and firm at 45.

"I'm sorry, Grant." She sat down in the empty easy chair next to him. She reached over, touched his knee. Her hand sat on his leg, soft and light. "You asked me last night what I thought of your photos. It was late, you know I'm tired at night, even more so last night after the faculty meeting, and tonight again after meeting with parents. You want the truth, don't you? I like your landscapes, but these didn't, they just didn't strike me as gallery material."

Grant sat quietly next to Pauline. She got up and went to eat her soup. The light from the kitchen fell onto the living room floor, where it made a long, yellow rectangle on the blue carpeting. He could hear her in there, stirring her soup and then pouring it into a bowl, shaking a bottle of dressing for her salad. She sat down at the kitchen table, opened the newspaper and spooned soup into her mouth, turning the pages of the Bulletin, reading the arrest reports of the folks in this city she and Grant had come to call home, where they'd decided to stay while raising their son through junior high and high school and now into college.

Miles Davis stopped playing. Grant sat still in the quiet of the study, his glass of red wine next to him.

"Judd Cameron got picked up for DUI again," Pauline yelled out. "He's got to be headed for jail this time, what is it, his fourth? Fifth? Geez oh man, and he's only twenty-four years old, a has-been high school quarterback, flunks and drinks his way out of college. I blame his dad."

Pauline stayed in the kitchen for an hour or so, then moved to the front porch, where she liked to sit in a folding lawn chair and watch the neighborhood. Finally, she was back in the room with Grant. She stood in front of him, looking down at him. She got down on her knees, so that her face was level with his. In the dull light, her blue eyes were dark.

"You're a good photographer, Grant. I assume that's what you're mad about, what I said last night. OK. Maybe I'm wrong. Submit the landscapes and see what happens. But you asked me. You asked me. You know I'm honest."

Grant stared back at her, then blinked.

"Well, I know you can hear me," she said, "or you wouldn't have had the stereo playing. Whatever I did, I'm sorry. C'mon upstairs and we'll talk about it."

THE SILENT TREATMENT

Grant listened to her footsteps go up the stairs. Then he heard the water running through the bathroom pipes, which meant that Pauline was doing her teeth. Her life had always been a routine, everything done in the same order in the same way every day. Right now, she would have just changed out of her sweats and into her sleeping shirt. Then she washed her face. Then she did her teeth. Then she sat on the toilet one last time before sleep.

Sure enough, Grant heard the flushing water upstairs. He stood up, climbed the steps, stripped to his underpants and got under the sheets just before Pauline came into the bedroom. Sometimes he did his teeth right after hers; other times, he watched television until the yawns came. When they made love, he always did his teeth afterwards.

Pauline slipped under the covers next to him. The room was quiet, the television off.

"Tired?" she said.

Grant stared at the ceiling in the darkness.

Pauline sighed. She reached over; he felt her hand slide across his stomach, her fingers slip inside his underwear. She touched him, caressed him, until he was ready. Then she pulled off her panties and tugged on Grant, urging him on top of her. They made love in the darkness, then Grant rolled off and lay on his back.

"Feel better?" she said after awhile. "Grant?" She jabbed him lightly with her elbow.

"What is it then? Is it work again? What the hell is it? Sex? Is this about me and sex, Grant? Is it that old argument?"

Pauline sat up. She looked at him; he could feel her eyes on him. He stared through her eyes, beyond her.

She put her arm across him, pushed her fingernails lightly across his stomach. "I know, I think I know. You're bored with your life. Feel like you missed out on your goals. Look. We'll get there. We've got some college expenses for David. We set some financial goals, remember? Once David's through with his school, then, you can quit and do your photography. You can spend the rest of your life taking pictures. The galleries can wait two, three more years, can't they? Is that it? What? How can I fix it if you won't tell me, Grant?"

She sighed again. Grant felt her eyes close. Pretty soon, she snored softly. She always fell asleep on her back. Grant couldn't sleep on his back, always awoke with a loud snort when he fell asleep on his back. He slept best on his left side, against Pauline's back, with his arm around her, holding her breast in his hand. He sat up. The corner streetlight shone into the bedroom, like white moonlight. He could see Pauline's face, the pulse of her neck. Her cheek bones were a soft outline in the dim light. Her lips were thin, pressed together; she breathed through her nose as she slept. Her right fingers twitched for a moment; she shuddered, opening her mouth, her white teeth showing in the darkness of the room. She had a high forehead that showed more when she lay on her back, her hair falling away from her face. Her chin was square and firm; her complexion was clear except for a small set of seven or eight freckles just below each eye. It was a friendly face, one he'd never tired of seeing, never dreaded awakening to, was usually pleased to see come into a room or through the kitchen door after a work day. She smiled easily, her thin, oval eyes crinkling at the edges. He could tell her mood from her face, stern when she was angry, her eyes alert when she was telling him about her day, her eyes thin and angry when she was complaining about a slight by a neighbor or coworker. Grant studied her face now, like it could be a photograph waiting to be taken, depending for its mood on the F-stops and shutter speeds he might use to get the image he wanted – a shadowy, sleepy figure; a dim, soft-focus repose. He had always loved the way he could create or alter a mood with the turn of a lens or the timing of an aperture; the way he could control his world with the dials and settings of a camera – control that went only so far and had no lasting effect on health or happiness, that could not stop time or slow down dying, make the slaughter and lying in every day's news go away. But with his camera, Grant could create a viewpoint, an effect, could manipulate and capture the sequences and consequences of the world and its life.

In the middle of the night, everything was quiet beyond Grant's and Pauline's bedroom window. Pauline awoke, felt Grant sleeping next to her. She reached over and gently shook him awake.

"Grant."

He opened his eyes and saw her, looking at him.

"Are you OK?"

Grant didn't answer.

"Oh geezus. Stop this, please? Please?"

She was still watching Grant when he rolled over, closed his eyes and went back to sleep.

II

All I want is blackness. Blackness and silence.

– Sylvia Plath

Grant sat at the round table on the newspaper's patio with Pauline and Walt. He listened to Pauline make her explanation to Walt.

"I appreciate you letting him take some sick leave for this," Pauline said. Walt leaned his head back and blew a stream of smoke toward the sky. The smoke hung in the still air a moment; someone pushed through the door and the cafeteria sucked it inside like a ghost vanishing into its nether world.

"No big deal," Walt said. "He hasn't taken any time off since I've known him, other than vacations. And I had to fight him to take those."

"There was that time I had to go in for those tests," Pauline said. "He took a couple days then."

"Oh yeah, that." Walt stirred his cup of coffee with a plastic stick. He had a reddish-brown moustache that was thick, like brush bristles, above his full upper lip. His cheeks were puffy, his eyes bloodshot beneath thick, dark brown eyebrows that covered his deep eye sockets like furry awnings. His chin was gristly with whiskers. It was a face that had thickened and widened over the years, from Walt's young days as a cub photographer, when he eagerly shot high school football games on Friday nights and then arose on Saturday mornings to shoot a visiting dignitary or to visit a small-town festival and photograph children laughing on the merry-go-round. He'd been at this paper all of his life, through one marriage and well into a second, recording the city's important historical events – new buildings going up, old ones coming down, fires, graduations, championship basketball games, presidential and senatorial visits, elections – until now, having worked his way up to photo editor. His responsibility now was to assign the city's pictorial history to the five photographers who worked for him. He took his role as photo-historian seriously, talking about its importance, about the pictures of the day and their significance in the greater panorama of community life and events, over beers with the newspaper librarian, Madeline Coons, at Mario's Tavern, where they met nightly after work.

"They gave him all the tests," Pauline was telling Walt. She'd worn a dress for the occasion of driving her husband to his job and fully explaining his situation to Walt, more than she'd been able to tell him over the telephone the day after Grant stopped talking. The silence had filled hers and Grant's house for nearly two weeks now. "They can't find a thing wrong with him physically. His heart's good. His brain checked out. Blood was fine. The doctor thinks maybe it's something psychological, so I guess that's our next step."

Walt glanced at Grant, whose eyes were on him.

"But the doctor said he could work?"

Pauline nodded. "Oh yeah. He checked out his reflexes, muscles, everything. Only thing is, he won't talk to anybody."

"Won't, or can't?"

Pauline shrugged. She looked at Grant, who was still gazing at Walt's face, at the wrinkles around his eyes, at the creases in his forehead where, with the right aperture and timing settings, the small shadows could be made into parallel horizontal charcoal scratches.

"I guess he can't," she said. "I mean, if he could talk, he would, wouldn't he? I mean,

Walt, there have been times, you know, we've had our quarrels like any married couple. He's just clammed up on me, sometimes for a couple days even, but then he's back just like before and we talk things out."

"It's none of my business, Pauline, but did you guys quarrel before this?"

"No. Everything was fine. I mean, maybe a small flareup a couple days before, but it was over. At least I thought it was." She glanced again at Grant, who was staring across the room now.

Nick Brewster, Tracy Berringer and Budd Sinclair Ralston were at a neighboring table, listening to Ralston talk about the latest investigative package he was working on – a series of stories on the children of immigrant migrant workers. Ralston's parents had named him after a couple of literary figures, one fictitious – Billy Budd – the other real – Upton Sinclair. Both professors, one of English, the other of journalism, they apparently figured the mixture of names would guarantee a writing career for their son – and he'd made good, so far. Or so he'd told gatherings at the Friday night beer and wine sessions at the Club Cafe downtown where reporters, lawyers, politicians, artists and the city's intelligentsia and hangers-on gathered. Under the byline B. Sinclair Ralston

– he liked the first-initial, full-middle-name moniker, like F. Scott Fitzgerald used – he'd won three consecutive first-place state Associated Press Association awards for investigative reporting. He'd published some freelance non-fiction pieces in a couple of regional magazines and had placed some short fiction in small, but important, literary magazines. And he'd begun working on weekends on a novel, with a plot he refused to divulge, other than a few tantalizing hints – that it was a crime novel but not in the pure sense because its characters had more depth and were more complex than the typical crime novel characters. There would be existential elements, though nothing of the depth of Sartre or Camus, of course.

"I guess since he can't or won't talk, I'll just have to shuffle his assignments," Walt said. "Should be no problem. I have plenty of lab work; he knows his way around the dark room and computer."

Pauline furrowed her eyebrows but kept her smile.

"No pictures?" she said. "He's a shooter, Walt."

"I know. But how's he supposed to get cutline information, you know, IDs, the who-what-why-when stuff that goes at the bottom of the pictures?"

Ralston's face was pale beneath hair that was dark and combed straight back over his head in neat, thin rows like black straw. His hair shone from the oil that held it in place. The juxtaposition of the black hair and black wire-rim glasses over narrow, dark eyes with the long, thin, white, whisker-clean face was like the contrast in a photo of pure white marble illuminated by a spotlight in the black of night; Ralston's photo would look wonderful someday on the dust cover of a novel, a deep, psychological and philosophical thriller that people would talk about in bars and at library reading clubs, that they would shake their heads over because of the various clues and hints and ambiguities of the novel that would leave them wondering what it all meant but sure that it carried messages of vast importance and significance. Ralston smirked, then opened his mouth into a wide, white smile that glistened with teeth as strong and clean and straight as the tines of a gleaming silver fork. He nodded at some point that Tracy Berringer, one of the newspaper's photographers, had just made. Her eyes looked at Ralston with awe mixed with respect – wide eyes that would eagerly devour every word of Ralston's novel, that would read these words and transmit

THE SILENT TREATMENT

them to a brain that had already stamped the work as that of a genius.

Grant was going to be an artist once, was going to produce black-and-white studies of humanity that would prompt observations, questions and ponderings similar to those of Ralston's novel when it was completed and published, as it no doubt would be with the talent and a name and parental connections like Ralston possessed.

"I imagine I'll find some things he can shoot," Walt said to Pauline. They stood; Grant followed their cue and stood up with them. The trio walked through the courtyard, where bushes and saplings and a small lawn of rolling hills were surrounded by the new, clean red brick of the newspaper building. The sun shone on them as they walked along the sidewalk that led back to the building that housed the editorial department and main lobby.

The lobby was filled with canvases on easels and wall hangings, an exhibit of paintings. The newspaper publisher, having ordered frequent editorials on the value of art and creative thinking in the community and in the education of the community's children, decided to back up his words with actions when he opened the new newspaper building north of the city. He sponsored a rotating exhibit of art, from the work of the local painting guild, which was on display now, to tapestries and weavings and quilts and ceramics produced by various area artists. Occasionally, he offered the works of his own photo staff. The stuff was displayed tastefully around the large, atrium-like lobby, with its domed, glass ceiling that allowed filtered, green light to enter the room with its large clay pots and planters brimming with flowers and small trees.

Walt walked Pauline to the front door.

As his wife and boss made their small talk – Walt had a son studying architecture, and he was doing fine; Pauline was concerned about the state legislature's trend away from the teaching of music and the arts in the schools – Grant studied a water color depiction of red and white geraniums in a wooden planter on a country front porch. The blossoms were delicate, casting fuzzy shadows onto the edges of the planters and then down onto the cement ledges on which they perched. On the next easel, a set of purple and blue pansies posed surrounded by vines that climbed a wooden fence post and rail; they grew in rich, dark soil, and they sweat drops of silver morning dew.

The water color renderings were blurry

photo-like images of the spring flowers they represented.

"If it helps, Pauline, you're not the only one he did that to," Walt said at the door that led to the visitors' parking lot. "He'd get mad at work once in awhile and go off into this silent thing for a day or two." The photo chief glanced at Grant, who was still studying the painted flowers. "Now that I think about it, Grant didn't say anything when he left work that day. He'd shot that teenage auto fatality that morning and left me the prints of his photos. I thought it was strange; he usually pokes his head into my cubbyhole and says goodbye or something and lets me know the pictures are in the daily computer photo file. But that day, he just left."

"That girl who died in the accident?" Pauline said.

Walt nodded.

"That was awful," Pauline said. She looked at Grant. "See you tonight, OK?"

She and Grant, standing a few feet from Walt, looked at each other for a couple of moments, then Pauline turned. Grant watched her as she strode to the parking lot, then Walt touched his arm and motioned him to come along with him.

They sat down in Walt's small office. His desk had a few printouts of photos already taken that day, for the next morning's paper. Others would find their way to his desk throughout the day; he would sort through them and select the strongest offerings for the 4:30 budget meeting, when the various department editors and Walt gathered with the newspaper's editor to pitch their stories and photos.

"Sit down, Grant." Walt motioned to the chair across from his desk; he sat down in his chair behind the desk. On the wall next to him, a drawing of a girl, just like the Vargas girls in the old Playboy magazines, hung above a calendar that said it was April. She wore a pink sweater that was tight over a pair of pointy, full boobs and beneath wide, doe-like brown eyes and a shoulder-length mane of hair. Her cheeks were red, like her lips, which were partially parted in a come-and-get-me kind of pout. She wore a tight black skirt that curved down to the middle of her calf, where nylon hose finished off her long legs, all the way into shiny black high heels.

Walt laced his fingers together on his desk and peered at Grant.

"What's this all about, buddy?" he finally said.

Grant peered back at Walt without expression.

"C'mon. You wanna talk about it?"

Grant didn't appear to want to discuss things with Walt.

"Things OK at home?"

Grant watched Walt talk.

"C'mon. You can nod your head, can't you?"

Grant didn't nod.

"It's about this place, isn't it? Like I told Pauline, I remember now. You clammed up that Friday before you went home. You came in from your assignments, downloaded your pictures, then poof. You were gone. Look, buddy, I'm sorry I took you off some of the daily stuff. I'm gettin' pressure, y'know? The publisher wants to increase ad lineage; we gotta take more pictures for advertising. That's life in the newspaper world now. It's all about ad lineage. That, and crap for the web site."

Walt poked an unlit cigarette into his mouth, like it was a piece of unchewed gum. "Goddam I hate this no-smoking policy. Used to be you could light up anywhere in the newsroom and just keep working. Now, you take it outside. You ever see those people out there, smoking?

Check ' em out. The women, they look like hookers, standing out there, leaning against the wall with their cigarettes."

A shaft of sunlight shone into the room through the picture window that separated Walt's office from the main newsroom, itself enclosed in glass walls that looked out onto the well-kept lawn and flowers of the newspaper park. The sunlight landed on Walt's head, highlighting the streaks of silver just above his ear.

"It's not like your pictures were any worse than anybody else's. You just seemed like a logical guy to throw the ad stuff to cuz, you know, your stuff takes less finish work. You bring it in clean. You understand what the ad guys want in the pictures. It ain't that you didn't give me what I want in news photos. Is that what this is all about then?"

Grant blinked and continued listening.

"All right, listen," Walt said. "I'm gonna throw some stuff at you that won't require talking. Stuff where you'll work with the writers on their projects, that way they can take care of the cutlines and you don't have to worry about asking questions and talking to people. Ralston's at the point in his immigration project where he's ready for a shooter to accompany him full-time.

I was gonna put Tracy on it, but she'll live. She loves this stuff, y'know?"

Walt sucked on his unlit cigarette and scratched his belly, which stretched out his white, button-down shirt just above the shiny silver belt buckle.

"Not that you don't love that kind of stuff. You can do picture pages too, y'know? Fires. Mood pieces. Some stand-alones that don't require interviews. We'll make this thing work, buddy, don't worry."

Walt twirled the cigarette in his mouth, took it out and looked at it, then poked it back between his lips.

"Aw Grant, I ain't gonna shit you. It's all about money, that's all it is. Y'know, thirty years ago, when I was just startin' out, we took pictures. Real goddam pictures of people doing things, cops makin' busts, people doing their work, traffic jams, fires. We still do that, but not so much, y'know? We're goddam photojournalists now. Y'know why I threw the ad stuff at you? Cuz you did it without complaining. Tracy, she gets all in a huff, y'know?" He mimicked her voice. "'Hey man, I didn't attend the New York Institute of Photography to take pictures of cars for sale.' And then the stuff she turns in, it's crap. Don't tell her this,

this is between you and me, OK?"

Grant said nothing.

"Oh yeah. Of course. I mean, you get your voice back, keep this to yourself. I don't blame you for bein' pissed, I'm pissed too at this whole goddam setup, at what we're becoming. We're all for sale now, y'know? The old man, before the kid took over the paper, the old man wanted to make money all right. But he wanted to do a newspaper too. I don't know what the kid wants – listen to me, callin' him a kid. He's goddam forty years old and I'm calling him a kid. But that's what the hell he is. Christ, listen to me, are you listening to me?"

Grant looked straight into Walt; Walt stared back.

Walt looked around the room, then back at Grant. He lowered his voice, barely above a whisper. "I'll tell ya what he is, buddy. He's a goddam prostitute. That's what he is. New ad account walks into this place, first thing the publisher does is spread his legs. He doesn't know a goddam news story from his ass. That's what he is, and we're all pimpin' for him."

Walt took another, long suck on his cigarette.

"Go out and see what kind of stand-alones

you can find, OK? Keep the radio on in case I need to contact you. Otherwise, I'll see you back here around three or so; bring me something featureish for the front of the lifestyle section. Oh Christ, wait, I forgot, we got a photoillustration out there tomorrow, drawing of a playground pointing out the hazards of all the equipment. Y'know, kids can hang themselves on improperly hung swings; they can break their goddam necks on some of that stuff. We got a big story on the dangers of the playground. Christ, I can remember when we did real journalism, when you'd turn to the features section and find a reader about some guy who makes and plays his own guitars and drinks rum out of the bottle while he plays the blues on them, real blues like Robert Johnson played, you know, interesting people kind of stories. Now we tell people how dangerous their goddam playgrounds are, what kind of toys they oughta buy at Christmastime. We're trying to be their goddam parents, buddy, instead of telling them the news and just givin' em' a good goddam read. Go see what you can find out there, we'll find a place for it. Tomorrow I'll hook you up with Ralston and we'll get going on his project. You're still gonna shoot some ads now and then, but I don't blame you for bein' pissed about this, God knows I am. Me, I'm headin' to the john and take a healthy crap."

Walt stood up, stuffed his cigarette into a green, tin ashtray and left Grant sitting at his desk. Grant went to the photo supply room, grabbed a camera, the keys to one of the Jeep Cherokees and headed outside to find Walt a feature photograph for the next morning's newspaper, maybe some flowers, something colorful like those paintings in the lobby, something that the cutline information would be in an encyclopedia, maybe a detail photo of a praying mantis on a twig, or a turtle basking in the sun at the pond.

III

Silence is the great teacher, and to learn its lessons you must pay attention to it. There is no substitute for the creative inspiration, knowledge, and stability that come from knowing how to contact your core of inner silence.

– Deepak Chopra

Magazines – People, Field and Stream, National Geographic – stood on end in a rack against the wall of the psychiatrist's office. Grant studied the offerings, then picked up a tattered Sports Illustrated and a fresher National Geographic and carried them back to his seat next to Pauline.

The back-page essay in Sports Illustrated was a diatribe against the commercialism of the college bowl games which, according to the writer, had sold out to the dot.coms and the financial institutions and to any other conglomerate that bid the highest price. Long gone are the Rose Bowl, the Orange Bowl, the Sun Bowl and all of the other traditional bowls, replaced by bowl games with the names of companies in front of them. The players? Well, they wear sporting goods emblems, and everybody knows they're only in the bowl games to better their status in the pro draft. College football isn't about emotionalism any more, it's about bucks and business, the writer wrote.

Yeah. Like life.

Grant glanced around the room. A man in blue jeans and a tan work shirt with its sleeves rolled up to the elbows sat in one corner, thumbing through Popular Mechanics. Grant studied his face, or what showed of it through the thick, kinky red beard that covered as much of his facial skin as oceans do a world globe. His eyes were dark, staring through narrow slits. His ears protruded from his head like a couple of handles on a jug. His orange hair hung down to his shoulders and joined up with the beard to make a solid continent of unruly, wavy orange. His nose, also red, and pocked, was an island of skin in the mass of hair. The man's eyes met Grant's; Grant thumbed through the National Geographic. He found a color photo of an Atlantic puffin, its thin black wings spread as it flew in clear, stop motion directly toward the lens of the camera. Soft white snowflakes, some of them more clearly defined than the blurred cotton balls suspended in a soft blue sky, swirled around the penguin-type face, orange beak and orange webbed feet of the bird. "Bright beaks and feet signal the breeding season for Atlanic puffins on Horneya Island," read the cutline. "The birds' colors dull for winter. Puffins in summer and winter coloration look so different they were once thought separate species." As usual for the magazine, which was the Carnegie Hall for photojournalists, the picture was a well-rendered capturing of nature, of an altering world and environment – indeed, Grant had mused, the magazine frequently now was a visual archive of disappearing species and landscapes due to the changing, warming planet.

He thumbed through the ads – cars, cameras, faucets, products, in dazzling color, still-lifes of the shimmering Great American Commercial. Grant remembered some of his own creative commercialism. One he'd especially liked was a photo-illustration of a giant glass vial, with three men trapped inside. The headline said: "Cooking with Herbs." And each of the men trapped in the glass container was named Herb – a lawyer, a local chef and a school teacher; each of them shared a favorite recipe: spaghetti with marinara sauce from the lawyer, grilled salmon from the chef, meatless meat loaf from the teacher. The page had been a big hit in the office.

"That's what a food page ought to be," proclaimed Ralston. "Tasty."

"Nice illustration," said Walt. "I'm gonna try that salmon shit this weekend. Does beer go with salmon?"

"Could have used a little bit more shading behind the container," Tracy said. "But hey, not bad."

The editor pasted a tear sheet of the page on the bulletin board in the mail room, with a scrawl across the top: "Damn fine work! – Derek Fisher."

As though every reporter, editor, photographer and clerk in the place didn't recognize Fisher's handwriting.

"Mr. Baker?" The voice came from behind the window that separated the waiting room from the receptionist's desk.

"That's us," Pauline said.

"Dr. Clevenger will see you now," said the woman behind the window.

Grant followed his wife to the corner of the room, where a door was opening; he glanced at the receptionist's head as he walked by, saw blonde hair that curled in just below the ears, a row of black roots along the part down the middle of the top of her head, a pair of purple frame glasses perched on a bird's beak of a nose. Another woman, this one all in white like a nurse, met them with a smile at the door and beckoned for them to follow her. She pushed open another door; Grant saw a man with wavy black hair sitting behind a big wooden desk. The only items on the desk were a laptop computer with its lid closed, a square glass paper weight, a closed manila file folder, a yellow legal pad and a writing pen.

"Mr. and Mrs. Baker?" Clevenger stood up. He held out his hand for the first taker; Pauline grabbed it, pumped it twice, then let it go. The doctor turned and offered it to Grant, who also shook it a couple of times. The man's grip was weak, his hand sweaty.

They all sat down. The doctor opened the manila folder and studied its contents for a couple of minutes. Grant watched him, watched the psychiatrist's eyes move from left to right as the doctor scanned the notes. Doctors always do this. They wait until you're in the room, then they study the file – something they could have done on their own time, while you were still waiting. Grant always had to go to a shoot prepared, even the advertising ones, knowing what the subject would be, what the story or the ad was about, what the reporter or assigning editor or ad rep was looking for. Doctors were never prepared – a state of being that seemed to Grant to work in an inverse ratio to the salary: the more money earned, the less prepared the worker.

A big framed poster hung on the wall behind the doctor, who wore a thin black tie on top of a light blue dress shirt. It depicted Rodin's The Thinker, situated just beyond a wooden crate, as though the statue were pondering that crate and its contents. Bold, black letters at the bottom of the poster, which was covered with glass and framed in aluminum-colored metal, said: "Think Outside The Box." On the wall to the doctor's left hung his school diplomas. A grandfather clock ticked at the opposite wall.

"You were referred by Dr. Stingly," the psychiatrist finally said. His voice was like an oboe, thin but melodic, a pleasant voice. Grant had wondered sometimes what his own voice sounded like to people; he'd heard it on a tape recorder a few times, and it sounded nothing like he sounded to himself. What did Dr. Clevenger's voice sound like to Dr. Clevenger? A clarinet? A cornet?

"He says you've lost your ability to speak," the psychiatrist said. "And he says it's nothing physical."

The psychiatrist raised his eyebrows, without lifting his head, and looked at Grant, then at Pauline. He clasped his hands together, then unclasped them and drummed his right thumb on the desk top for a moment.

"Tell me when this first happened," he said, looking at Pauline. She wore a blue skirt and white blouse, with silver hoop earrings that made her black hair look blacker while complementing her few streaks of silver. Pauline knew how to dress.

"I came home from work one Wednesday night, there he was in the study, listening to some of his jazz," she said. "I thought at first he was just in another one of his moods. He gets mad at me sometimes and just shuts up. It's usually gone by the next morning. But not this time. The next morning, when he still wasn't talking, I called him and me in sick and made him stay home."

Grant enjoyed listening to Pauline's voice. It was soft, smooth and low, like a cello.

"You just got home from work," the doctor said. "What do you do?"

"I teach. Fourth grade."

The doctor nodded, made a note on his legal pad.

"And what does Mr. Baker do?"

"He's a newspaper photographer."

The psychiatrist made another note.

"Oh. And a couple years ago, he started his own business part-time," Pauline said. "He shoots graduation pictures and an occasional wedding."

"Uh huh." The doctor made another note. "You say he sometimes gets moody. What about?"

"Sex," Pauline blurted.

"Sex?"

"He thinks I don't like it. I do. But he doesn't believe that."

"What makes him think you don't like it?"

Pauline shrugged. "He just thinks that when I'm too tired or just not in the mood."

"So how often do you have sex?"

"Are these questions necessary?" Pauline said. "I don't think this is about sex."

The doctor nodded. "Any question I ask is necessary. I'm not prying. I'm trying to discover why your husband has gone silent." He smiled, drummed his thumb a couple more times, then glanced at Grant.

Grant glanced back.

"Can you smile at me, Grant?" the doctor said.

Grant stared at the psychiatrist.

"Nod your head if you can hear me."

Grant nodded his head.

"Good," the psychiatrist said. "He understands, at least. Raise your right arm for me, Grant."

Grant lifted his right arm, then put it back on his lap.

"Oh, he goes to work," Pauline said. "He can do everything he's done before, even the sex. He just can't, or won't, talk."

"Interesting choice of words," the psychiatrist said. "Can't, or won't. Which is it, Grant?" the doctor said, suddenly looking back at Grant. "Can't, or won't?"

Grant returned the doctor's gaze.

"How often during the week do you and your husband engage in sexual activity?" the doctor said, returning his eyes to Pauline.

"I don't know. I don't keep track. I'd say two or three."

"Really? Wow." He scratched another note. Grant watched the doctor's hand push the pen across the paper. His nails were clean and closely cut, his hands soft, uncalloused.

"Does that seem like a lot to you, Mrs. Baker?"

"No. But he never seemed to think it was

enough. That, and he wanted me to do other things, besides just the sex."

"Other things?"

"Oral sex. Or he wanted me to pose naked in unusual places."

"Did you do these things?"

"No. Doctor, I love my husband. But I think sex is just that. It's sex, an act of love, of intimacy, between two people. It's not voyeurism. It's not anything else. It's not asking a partner to do something she's uncomfortable doing. It's making love."

The doctor wrote more notes.

"Who usually initiates the sexual activity?" he asked.

"He does."

"Do you ever?"

Pauline thought a moment. "Yes. When we've gone to bed, it's usually me who starts up."

"Then when does he initiate sex?"

"When we're anywhere but the bedroom. In the kitchen or living room. On the front porch at night. Then he asks me if I'd like to go upstairs."

"And do you?"

"Unless I'm busy."

"How long does sex usually last between

you?"

Pauline's face reddened. "I don't understand the significance of this. My husband has stopped talking. He hasn't stopped having sex. We had sex the first night he came home not talking, and we've had it on a regular basis since then. OK?"

Clevenger put his pen down. He folded his hands and looked across the desk into Pauline's face.

"Mrs. Baker, I am not prying. I'm trying to help your husband. I asked what you two fought over, when you fight, you immediately said sex. That seemed the likely avenue to explore. I can't ask your husband these questions, so I have to ask you."

Pauline nodded. The redness faded from her face. "All right. I just don't understand all the questions. I don't understand what the length or frequency of the sexual act has to do with him shutting up."

The doctor nodded.

"There are other times he gets moody," Pauline said.

"Money? Do you fight over money? That's a common cause of marital disagreement."

She shook her head. "No. I've always handled the finances, and he's never complained. He gets angry about things at work. He comes home, sometimes he won't talk to me all night because of something that's gone wrong at work."

"The old silent treatment. In the movies, it's always the wife who does it to the husband." The doctor wrote another note. He was a thin man, maybe five foot ten. Grant watched the doctor's face. His pale skin hadn't been exposed to much sun. There was one window in the room, so any pictures likely would have to be shot with artificial lighting, depending on the time of day. He could use a white screen for bounce if he wanted to create starker shadows; the doctor's face would harbor a few shadows, below his high cheek bones, beneath his long, thin nose, under his sharp chin. His eyes were green, under thick black eyebrows. His skin, cleanly shaved, carried a couple of small craters from a young bout with acne; he wore gold wire-frame glasses. His hair was plush like a television evangelist's, combed straight back in black waves. The most marked feature of his head area, though, was his Adam's apple, which moved up and down his scrawny neck as he talked and swallowed.

"Grant wanted to do artistic photography when he was young," Pauline said. "He's been getting more and more frustrated, especially as his job has changed; I think he's starting to feel like he's failing in life."

The psychiatrist glanced at Grant, who sat still, his eyes intent on the doctor's head.

"Lately they've been having him shoot less news and sports and regular pictures and concentrate more on advertisements," Pauline said.

The doctor nodded. "And he doesn't like this?"

"Not in the least. He complains a lot – er, complained. Says this isn't why he got into the business. I'd say he's pretty angry about things right now, if that helps. But then, he always seems angry about something."

"Anything you know of that especially irked him, just before he went mute?" the doctor asked.

Pauline thought a moment. She looked at her husband, who was still studying the doctor. She shook her head. "Nothing. He'd gotten mad at me the night before, when I told him I didn't think his landscapes were gallery material. He's always wanted to show his work in a gallery, just never did."

The doctor jotted more sentences, then pushed his chair back from the desk.

"Mrs. Baker, I'm not a specialist in this particular disorder, but I've done some reading on it. From everything you've told me and from the little I know about the subject, this sounds like a condition called selective mutism. It would be a most acute case, if that's what it is – but from everything I've studied, that sure is what it sounds like."

Pauline raised her eyebrows. "Selective? What does that mean?"

"Well, it was first called elective mutism because researchers believed it was a voluntary, deliberate condition; but its name evolved from elective to selective, because they've now determined that it seems more haphazard than deliberate, and other factors seem to come into play. It is a condition in which the patient for some psychological or possibly physiological reason goes into a sort of shell, vocally. It's most frequent in children. They're afraid to speak up at school or in public, but they're often just fine at home."

"He's not a child," Pauline said.

Grant watched the doctor's head go up and down, his Adam's apple bobbing, as the psychiatrist and Pauline talked about him.

"Like I said, this would be a more acute version of the condition. I said it's most frequent with children, Mrs. Baker, not that it affects only children. It's a disorder that can and has affected any age, and it's characterized by the sort of symptoms evidenced in your husband's case. Researchers attribute this inability, or unwillingness, to verbalize to anxiety, or fear, or shyness, embarrassment or psychological trauma. They've linked it to severe anxiety and social phobia, but the exact cause isn't known – nor is a specific cure. I'm afraid I'm going to have to read up on it beyond that – or perhaps refer you to a specialist."

"Can't you hypnotize him or something?"

Clevenger grinned. "I'm not a hypnotist, Mrs. Baker. Please don't confuse my profession with what you see depicted on television."

"We don't watch television."

Clevenger erased his grin. "Mrs. Baker, I'd like you to let me have a few words alone with your husband."

"It's likely to be a pretty one-sided conversation," Pauline said. She stood up.

The doctor smiled. "Would you mind waiting in the next room? I think perhaps ten minutes."

Pauline returned the doctor's smile. "I'm sorry to be difficult, Dr. Clevenger. I guess I'm afraid. And confused. I mean, you imagine bad things happening to someone you care about, like cancer – not that I wish cancer on him. You know what I mean? This just came out of nowhere, selective something that I've never even heard of, and like you said, not much is known about it. I'm sorry."

Clevenger smiled again. "No need to be sorry. I understand. I've probably been a bit too clinical for you. We'll get him through this. He works. He eats. He functions. He sleeps, yes?"

"Yes."

"Just let me have him alone for a little bit."

Grant and Clevenger watched Pauline leave the room.

Clevenger leaned back in his chair and rested his head against the back support, so that his Adam's apple became all the more prominent, like a small light bulb buried beneath his skin. He stared at Grant, who stared back. They watched each other for about a minute.

"Grant," Clevenger said. "Tell me what's troubling you."

Grant did not respond.

"You can talk to me here," Clevenger said. "It's OK. Whatever happens in here is between me and you and nobody else. I am ethically bound to keep anything you tell me, or the fact that you speak at all, in this room. I will not, cannot, tell anyone else, not even your wife. Do you understand? Nod if you do."

Grant nodded.

Clevenger tore a yellow sheet from his note pad and pushed it, with a pen, across the desk.

"Write down any questions, or a sentence, for me," he said.

Grant looked at the pen, then back at Clevenger.

"Can't write either, eh?" the doctor said. "Can you smile?"

Grant sat still.

"Nod again," Clevenger said.

Grant nodded.

The doctor sighed.

"Is this about work, Grant? Is it a general funk you're in? Can you speak if you wish? Nod if I'm right."

Grant's head did not move.

"Is it about you and your wife? I'll say again, anything you tell me stays in here. I know you can hear me, I know you understand me, I know that you can nod. Is it related to your wife? Nod your head yes if it is, no if it isn't."

Grant stared at the doctor's Adam's apple,

which seemed to be alive all by itself, which was like a bird trapped in his throat like words were trapped in Grant's. He shook his head no.

"Would you tell me in words if you could? Please respond with a nod."

Grant peered back at the doctor.

"Fascinating." The doctor wrote a couple of sentences in his legal pad.

"Grant, is this about sex or intimacy with you and your wife?"

Grant shook his head no.

"Is she right, that you believe she doesn't like sex?"

Grant nodded yes.

"But that's not what this is about?"

No.

"Grant, do you love your wife?"

A quick nod yes.

"Are you having an affair?"

No.

"Because you know, Grant, there's nothing wrong with that. I mean, our society has piled so much guilt association onto the sexual act, even thoughts about sex, that things as simple as affairs, impotence, lack of interest in sex have caused psychological distress, if not trauma. I'm a Freudian, basically, as you likely have ascertained, Grant; but ever since the birth control pill, Freudian concepts have gone haywire. Sexual taboos related to unwanted pregnancies have shifted to other areas that take in morality and guilt. I realize, this is all simplistic, Grant."

The photographer imagined the doctor in a pose, capturing that Adam's apple in mid-bob as the doctor leaned back in his chair espousing Freudian and Jungian isms and theories and explanations about why people are all screwed up.

"I have one client, he was having an affair," the doctor said. "Guilt. He was all twisted up inside with guilt. You know why? Because he was developing feelings for his mistress. The affair began as simple sexual urgings between co-workers, and that was how it remained for some time – a once-a-week purely physical letting-go with no emotional involvement, based primarily in both partners being married to people who simply did not care about sex. But then when he started developing feelings for this woman, caring for her, that became a heavier emotional load than he'd intended. He didn't want to leave his wife, he just wanted a good lay now and then. I had him straightened out after three sessions; told him to drop the mistress and just find a good, reliable prostitute. Problem solved; he's happily married, his and his wife's investments and retirement are intact; their children won't be torn apart by divorce. Now, another man might develop guilt over the simple act of physical pleasure without the emotional involvement. My point is, Grant, that we've allowed our sexual fantasies and desires and acts to become so imbued with guilt that the whole goddam beauty of sex is lost along with creating some damned screwed up people. So, Grant, if sex is what's bothering you, give me a nod. Feel free to talk about it – er, to admit it. Now, is that part of what's bothering you?"

Grant shook his head no.

"Do you know what's bothering you? Are you feeling guilt?"

No response.

"Let me shift emphasis here a bit, Grant. Do you want to be able to verbalize again?"

Grant did not respond.

"Does it bother you that you can't talk, can't use your voice? Do you particularly care if you get it back?"

Grant looked at the doctor.

"Interesting." The doctor jotted another note. Then he laid his pen on the desk.

"Our time's about up, Grant. Y'know, it took me quite a while to develop my own freedom, my own attitudes about sex. I was raised in a highly restrictive environment. My father was uncomfortable talking to me about sex; he had his own guilty hangups about it from how he was raised, so my mother took over. Boy did she take over. She not only taught me about sex, but she taught me that it's sinful to even think about it with a woman beyond marriage – let alone to imbibe. My first time, in high school, I carried a cloud of guilt with me for weeks until I finally confessed it to my father – my father, because while I knew he was uncomfortable with it, he also was a man and would understand. First thing he did was go and tell my mother; and boy, there was a scene."

The doctor sighed as he gazed back at his youth. "Masturbation was taboo. Looking at dirty pictures was taboo. It took me a long time to overcome that early childhood training, Grant. I mean, now I can masturbate and enjoy the goddam act and the fantasies and the dirty pictures and all of the stuff that comes with a liberated notion of sex. My wife feels the same way. My first one didn't; she was an old-fashioned kind of girl. My mother loved her. But my second wife, now there's a liberated woman. My point is, Grant, if you're comfortable with your wife's sexual attitudes, and with yours, then that's fine. It sounds to me like she's having her own issues of guilt about sex; but if you're happy with your sexual state of being with your wife, we don't need to explore that. I'd like to set you up for another appointment though, in about two weeks, if that's all right."

Grant did not respond.

"Fine. I'll set it up and have my secretary give you a phone call to remind you a couple of days in advance. Meanwhile, Grant, I don't want you to be afraid of this. Chances are, it'll go away like it came – or it may not. I'll telephone a colleague who specializes in this sort of disorder. But Grant, get away from your sexual hangups. So many times, in adult psychological disorders, sex is at the bottom of the difficulty without people even realizing it until they've spent some time exploring their anxieties, working it through with professional therapy."

The doctor stood up. He extended his hand. Grant took it in his own, shook the doctor's hand, then turned and let himself out the door.

In the car, Pauline drove for a couple of blocks, listening to the music on the radio. At a red light, she looked across the seat at Grant. She reached over and patted his knee with her hand.

"I could have told that guy a lot of what he spent expensive time figuring out," she said. "I knew you could nod yes and no. I knew there was nothing wrong with your ability to reason. I don't think there's anything wrong with our sex life. Do you think this man can help you? The receptionist said you're going back."

Grant nodded.

"Grant, does our sex life bother you?"

He shook his head back and forth.

"Do you love me?"

He nodded.

"I love you, Grant. If you never talk again, I love you. Geez I talk enough for both of us anyway, don't I?" Pauline smiled. She leaned across the car, gave her husband a kiss on the forehead, then drove forward when the light turned green.

She drove Grant home, where he looked through his jazz collection, found a George Shearing album and put it on. Shearing, blind, could play better jazz missing one of his senses than most pianists could with all of theirs. You don't need eyes to play good music and you don't need a voice to take good pictures.

IV

Speak only if it improves upon the silence.

– Mahatma Gandhi

Ralston told Grant about his immigrant children series as they drove north toward Riverton. The road was a two-lane county thoroughfare that sliced through farmland, where tractors worked the soil, readying it for planting, and small groves of woodlands that had been spared the farmers' and land developers' machinery.

"I've got most of the paper research done," Ralston said. He shouted at Grant, as though the inability to speak was a symptom of deafness. "The statistics are sort of what you'd expect; we're looking at five aspects of the issue. Education, health care, crime, social factors like family life and housing, and economic status. Some of the stuff is a no-brainer. You know these guests of the American government – I got one university researcher calling them, in quotes, what they really are, which is economic slaves – are in the lower echelon of the economy. And I do mean lower echelon. Not only are they paid less than minimum wage, but they don't get benefits. These people are working jobs that nobody else wants, but like another university professor pointed out to me, they're also the ones who get criticized by all the right-wingers and isolationists for taking away jobs from unemployed Americans. But that's a bunch of shit, I can tell you, Baker; like this one broad told me with the state division of employment, no citizen's gonna get off his fat ass and give up his food stamps or unemployment or part-time salary to go work at a poultry farm cleaning up turkey shit or at the processing plant shoveling up turkey guts and blood."

Ralston punched a button on the Jeep Cherokee's radio and found a classic rock station. Smokey Robinson sang "Tears of a Clown" as the Cherokee's tires hummed over the newly paved, clean black highway.

"And it's the goddam kids who suffer," Ralston said. "And I got it all documented. I got so much shit on this subject I'll have to throw half of it away. The kids simply can't cut it in the schools, and these small rural school districts can't afford to hire the language specialists and intervention personnel to help them. Their parents are too fucking stupid and too tired from working all day to help the kids with their school work at night. I mean, you think latchkey kids in the city got it tough, they at least have some kind of support system – grandmothers, social workers, you know, a community that cares. But greater Riverton, all 10,000 citizens of that pristine Anglo-Saxon community, they not only don't give a shit about the migrant community – and remember, these folks are working here legally, and they're spending money in the local economy – they hate 'em to boot. Go into the bars in Riverton, and what're they complaining about? That their tax dollars are going to educate foreigners, to pay for their health care and to provide social services for them. So not only do they get slaves to do the work they don't want to do, they got ready-made targets for their bigotry. And it shows. You should see the crime statistics – and they ain't the kind of statistics you'd expect. Yeah, these immigrant kids do drugs all right, and a bunch of them drink their share of booze underage. But who do you think is selling them the drugs and booze? And what do you think the major crime is in Riverton?"

Ralston looked across the front seat at Grant, who was gazing out the open window at the fields, the groves of trees where birds soared above the tops of the foliage.

"Huh?" Ralston said.

Grant looked at Ralston.

"Vandalism," Ralston said. "Course, they never know who's doing it. But these immigrant workers' cars get smashed, their mail boxes torn down, their fences kicked in, their windows busted. I tell ya, Baker, this is Pulitzer Prize stuff. We're gonna need some good goddam pictures to help tell this story."

The disc jockey talked on the radio about a special appearance that radio station personnel would be making at a weekend health fair at the Crosstown Mall.

"Get your blood checked, have your blood pressure and cholesterol measured, and representatives from area hospitals will be on hand to answer your questions about health-care needs and the services they offer. And hey, while you're there, our own Abby Rhodes will be playing all your favorite oldies, from the Beatles to the Beach Boys, and register to win a new Hyundai. See you there."

"You won't see me there, pal," Ralston said to the radio. He pushed up the green sunglasses on his nose, leaned back and rested his left elbow on the sill of the open window. A breeze blew through the front of the car as the reporter and photographer sped toward Riverton.

Ralston smiled at the radio. "I'll be busy workin' on my own stuff this weekend."

Ralston glanced across the seat again. Grant was looking straight ahead through the windshield.

"I do my real writing on the weekends," Ralston said to Grant. "I get up at six in the morning, I write until 10 or so, break for breakfast, then I'm back at it for another couple hours. Do the same thing on Sunday. You're in your bed sawing logs, I've got my novel going. I average about 30 pages a weekend. I'm halfway through the sucker. Don't ask me to tell you what it's about though. I don't talk about my real writing. I'll gladly tell you about my newspaper writing, anything you want to know. But don't ask me about my novel writing."

Grant didn't ask Ralston about his novel writing. Instead, he gazed at Ralston's head. It seemed larger than most heads, with a wide, thick jaw and a forehead to match. His black hair flapped in the wind. Ralston's eyebrows moved up and down as he talked; his face was a lively one, never still, some part of it always moving – the mouth, the eyebrows, the hair, the whole head moving up and down as Ralston exclaimed about his novel.

"It's a crime yarn," he said. "That's about all you're going to get out of me. I plan for it to be the first of a series, about a university English lit professor who solves crimes. Man, think of the possibilities, the ironies and the allegories and the literary references – I mean, I borrow plots from the classics, take some liberties with various characters out of literature, you understand? But I can't tell you any more than that."

Ralston glanced over at Grant. "Not that I think you're going to blab it. That'd be kind of hard, with your condition, wouldn't it?" Ralston smiled. "It's just bad luck to talk about your writing, y'know? It's like I'd be sapping some of the life out of my characters if I talked about them out of context, out of their own world that I'm creating for them. I know, that sounds kind of weird to you, and I suppose I am. Writers are a weird bunch, I guess. They're paranoid, or they're alcoholics, or they're anti-social – they all have some kind of psychological hangup. That's what makes us creative, I guess. Anyway, I figure I'm tapping into unmined literary ore here, making a university professor a protagonist in a mystery series. But I'll tell you what, I've contacted a literary agent – friend of my folks – who thinks I'm onto something and wants to see my first draft when it's finished."

The Kinks sang "Lola" on the radio as they neared the Riverton exit.

"Damn," Ralston said as he began to slow the Cherokee. "I've probably gone and jinxed it there. I didn't mean to tell you about the agent; it's only speculation, see? Goddam it, I wish I'd learn to shut the hell up about my other writing."

He looked again across the seat at Grant. "You're just so easy to talk to, y'know? Damn good listener. Damn good. Listen, here's the plan when we get into town. The immigrant neighborhood is on the west side of town, just beyond the abandoned tire warehouse. I'm meeting a county social worker at the house of a woman who stays at home to take care of the kid. She's going to help me with translation – I don't speak Spanish. I'm going to interview this woman; I don't know her whole story, but I'll get it. She's the human-interest angle; the social worker set it up for me. Supposed to be quite a story; I guess the kid's autistic. The husband works all day at the turkey plant, then works a second job at night and they still can't pay their medical bills. The county health department and hospital help out a bit. These people are right on the edge, Baker; that's what this story's about. How's my tie look? Straight? Goddam I hate wearing these things. The day I get that novel published is the day I throw away neckties and goddam dress shirts and slacks for good and get out of this fuckin' newspaper business. Shit, all we are anymore is filler around the ads anyway, except the socially significant stuff we do now and then, like this series I'm on now – that's the only thing keeps me in the business. Anyway, I want you to take pictures of the house. Get the squalor, you know, the cracked walls, the peeling paint, the warped flooring. Go outside and shoot the yard and house. You might wanna get the woman and the kid too. But mainly I want the squalor. That's what this series is all about, squalor."

Grant checked the settings on his cameras – he'd brought a digital and a 35-millimeter. He still felt like he got better contrast and had better control over lighting and depth of field with film; but he would shoot both and probably use both.

"Then," Ralston said, "take the car out for a while. Take pictures of the neighborhood, the community center and the turkey farm and processing plant. I've called ahead, they're expecting you, they know about your, um, condition. They don't know what the series is about, other than a feature piece on their plant and its role in the community. They told me they'd let you take some interior shots of the plant; you'll likely have to use the zoom and shoot from a distance to get workers out on the farm, I mean the real workers doing the real shit work. Do the best you can. I told them to expect you. Just show them your press card, the rest is taken care of. Then meet me back at the house after about an hour."

They drove into Riverton and went down Main Street, past the Catholic church, then the primary business center – a self-serve gas station and convenience store on one corner, a doughnut shop on another, a small grocery store, and a bar. As Ralston drove through the four-way stop sign, Grant glanced into the open front door of the corner tavern, at the bent blue and red neon beer signs on the wall, the glistening glasses and bottles inside, the men and women sitting on the wooden stools. The soft twang of an electric guitar seeped out onto the sidewalk. They drove past a Methodist church and then into and through a residential neighborhood. The homes were primarily two-story, red brick or vinyl siding, with big, covered front porches, shade trees in the front and along the sides of the houses. The lawns were neatly clipped, the sidewalks swept. An elderly man and woman sat on one porch, she reading a magazine, he smoking a cigar and watching Grant and Ralston motor by. Ralston waved, the man nodded.

"Man," Ralston said. "Can you imagine spending an entire lifetime in a dipshit place like this? That's what most of these people do, they live here all their lives. Geez, what a life."

Actually, Grant had imagined living in a small town like this several times. Grant had spent much of his life imagining it to be other than it was; that's how Grant was, how he was raised. His parents had moved around; so he'd often imagined what life would be like in one place for a long time.

They came to the abandoned tire warehouse. Ralston turned right, then took another left, around to the back side of the warehouse; piles of tires littered the gravel and weed-infested back yard of the vacant building, which was separated from the street by a six-foot chain-link fence. They entered another, different neighborhood. Here, the houses were primarily frame and mostly one-story. Weeds mixed with crabgrass in the lawns. Broken glass littered the gutters next to the sidewalks, which were cracked and overgrown with grass and weeds.

Ralston watched the numbers on the houses, then pulled off and parked in front of a small house that was sided with gray slate shingles. A small elm tree struggled in the front yard; behind it, a rose bush and a couple of rows of pink petunias stood between the sparse lawn and the front of the house. The only porch was a set of cement steps and a small stoop.

"This be the place," Ralston said. "Can you believe, this is probably a mansion for these Mexicans. Man, I was down there once, you can't believe the way some of them live – in cardboard shacks, some of them, or places with wood siding filled with gaps, and dirt floors inside."

They got out of the car and approached the house. A woman pushed through the screen door. She wore a pair of tan slacks, a light yellow button-down shirt with the sleeves rolled up and a pair of sandals. Her dusty blonde hair was pulled into a bun, and she wore black frame glasses.

"You must be Mr. Ralston," she said, extending a hand to the reporter. "I'm Erma Metheny with the county office of social services."

Ralston took her hand, pumped it a couple times and introduced Grant.

"He can't speak," Ralston said.

"Oh, I'm sorry," the social worker said, taking Grant's arm and looking into his face. Grant gave her a blank stare.

"Don't worry, it doesn't affect his photographs any," Ralston said. "And he keeps a secret pretty well."

Ralston grinned at his joke. The social worker invited them inside. The living room was dimly lit; a woman in a flower-pattern dress stood in the doorway, backlit by the bright kitchen. She held a child in her arms, the child's head resting on her shoulders.

"This is Dora," the county worker said.

Ralston nodded. "I'm B. Sinclair Ralston," he said, raising his voice as though deafness were a symptom of poverty. Ralston always introduced himself with all three names.

"And this is my photographer," Ralston shouted, nodding his head in the direction of Grant, who had placed his camera bag on the floor and was busy screwing a lens into the 35-millimeter camera.

Grant ignored Ralston, the women and the child as he looked around the room. A small couch sat beneath the front window, which was covered with a light brown shade that was pulled down. A console color television set was in the corner opposite the couch; a commercial was on the screen, a man in a blue blazer and necktie, his blond hair greased back, shouting about the acres of used cars on his lot, all of them backed by a 30-day warranty. The color on the picture was sharp, with good contrast. The only other furniture in the living room was a floor lamp, with a broad lampshade that had been white at one time but that now was soiled and dusty. The wooden floor shone; the house was clean and tidy.

Behind him, the woman spoke Spanish, then Grant heard the county worker's voice. They and Ralston went into the kitchen.

Grant set to work. He followed the group into the kitchen, where something was simmering beneath the lid of a big, aluminum pot on a small, four-burner gas stove. A tiny, white refrigerator hummed next to the stove. The floor tiling was blue and clean.

There was no squalor to photograph in this house.

Grant situated himself opposite the mother, who continued to hold the child – a small boy with black hair and a pale face; he sucked on his thumb as he rested his head on the shoulder of his mother. Grant focused his camera on the woman's head. Sunlight streamed in through the window above the sink, illuminating her entire front. The three of them babbled in Spanish and English, Ralston asking questions, the two women answering, as Grant moved closer, then farther back, then closer again, concentrating on the woman's face; it was broad and clean, her black hair pulled behind her head into a tight pony tail that hung just below her broad shoulders. Her brown eyes were wide and round, her lips thin and naturally red. Her cheeks were fat. A couple of tiny, aqua-colored tear-drop-shaped earrings studded each of her lobes, which were wide and close to her head. Her nose also was wide; below it, thin facial hair spread in a line just above her lip, barely perceptible, like dark peach fuzz. Grant shot her from the side, with the boy's face in focus and the woman's facial outline a soft blur; the boy had his mother's eyes. His ears stuck out from the side of his head; his hair poked out in all directions from the top of his head. He sucked greedily at his thumb, resting his head on his mother's shoulder as she answered Ralston's questions.

Grant went outside and took pictures of

the house, including the dish antenna on the roof. The yard was clean, the scant lawn trimmed short. It was obvious the woman and her husband took pride in their home. Grant got into the Jeep Cherokee and drove through the neighborhood, eyeing the houses. He stopped and took a picture of an elderly man, his gray pony tail hanging out of a straw cowboy hat, dressed in denim overalls and a white T-shirt, a filterless cigarette dangling from his lips as he bent over a hoe and scratched weeds from a garden at the side of his house. Grant used a zoom lens and got close to the man's face, to the stubble that covered his chin, jaw and cheeks like a soft gray mud. Tiny wrinkles cracked the man's brown skin at the corner of each of his thin, gray eyes that sparkled in the midday sunshine. He stood up, took a long puff on his cigarette; the ash fell to the ground; he blew smoke into the air in front of him, then bent over and resumed his gardening. A couple of children approached Grant, one of them riding a battered red tricycle, the other pushing from behind. Dirt smudged their faces; their skinny legs looked like chicken drumsticks chewed clean of the meat poking out from baggy shorts. Each wore T-shirts, one white, one dark blue. The boy riding the tricycle wore a fresh, red-brown scab on his knee.

Grant aimed his camera at them; they smiled for a portrait as Grant moved from left to right and shot them from different angles until the wail of a mother from a few houses down summoned them back to their yards. Up and down the street now, women and children ventured from homes, silently watching Grant as he walked back to the Cherokee and drove farther down the road.

Grant stopped sporadically, took pictures of houses, of folks relaxing on their front porch steps, of a mother sitting in the shade of an oak tree as her toddler ran around a golden puppy that was chained to the trunk of the tree. At the end of the block, the water tower held up a big, blue bulb that contained Riverton's water. Grant climbed its ladder several rungs, then got on the back side of the ladder so that he faced the street and houses of the neighborhood. He used a long-focus lens and pulled the perspective of the street and its houses into a detail shot of Riverton's poor, immigrant neighborhood – a panorama of children, mothers, dogs, trees, houses and scrappy lawns like an album jacket for the music of a Mexican neighborhood. This would be the cover photo for the kickoff story of Ralston's series on immigrant children.

Back at the car, Grant stowed his camera

gear, got in and started back in the direction from which he'd come, toward the other end of Riverton and the Bingham Farms turkey processing plant, the village's primary industry and largest employer.

He drove past the bar, the churches, the convenience store and through a stop sign, which he saw too late in a side window as it flashed by. Next, in his rear-view mirror, he saw the flashing red and blue lights of the village's police cruiser. He pulled over and watched as the officer got out of his car, leaving the flashers going, and slowly walked toward the Cherokee, eyeing the vehicle carefully. Grant rolled down his window.

"Guess you didn't see the stop sign, huh?" the officer said. He wore brown uniform slacks with a black stripe, a brown shirt and a flat, trooper-style hat.

"Mind letting me take a look at your driver's license?"

Grant reached into his back pocket for his wallet, took it out and handed the license to the officer. The cop studied it for a while, then got out his ticket book and began writing.

"From out of town, huh?" the officer said as he wrote. His face, like his body, was stubby and fat. His black leather holster belt was cinched around a belly that hung over the belt. "What's with all the pictures you're taking of our village anyway? I got a few calls about you."

Grant did not respond.

"Don't be shy," the cop said. He wore a thin, black moustache below a pair of wide-set green eyes and above a pair of thick, red lips. His cheeks were flabby and hung down like the jowls of a hound dog. "Why all the pictures?"

Again, Grant said nothing. Instead, he reached into his wallet and took out his press card, which he handed to the officer.

"Ah, that explains everything," the officer said. "You're with the Bulletin. Or so this card says. And what is the Bulletin's interest in Riverton?"

Grant blinked at the officer.

"Y'know, there's no law that says you have to explain anything to me," the cop said. He sighed. "But it sure would help if you'd tell me why you're here. Fact is, you were trespassing on village property when you climbed up that ladder back there. You've been invading people's privacy, taking pictures of them minding their own business in their front yards. Now can't you just tell me what you're up to, I'll give you this ticket for running a stop sign and you can be on your way?"

Grant would not cooperate. He shook his head back and forth, slowly.

"Hang on," the officer said. He went back to his car and radioed into the station, where Chief Hanson was at the desk because Claire Longley had stepped out for her afternoon coffee.

"Chief," the officer on the scene said into the radio, "this guy who's been taking the pictures gave me a press card, says he's a photographer with the Bulletin. I got him going through a stop sign. He refuses to talk to me."

"Why?"

"Dunno."

Chief Hanson thought things over for a minute. "Why don't you bring him down here. I'll question him. We can't be too careful."

"You got it."

The officer walked back to the Cherokee. He handed Grant his driver's license and press card. "I need you to turn around and follow me back into town," he said. "The chief wants to meet you." He gave Grant a smirk, like the chief wanting to talk to him was no ordinary event, was, in fact, a rather important event in Riverton. Not everybody got invited to the chief of police's office in Riverton, the officer's smirk implied.

Grant followed the officer's squad car back to the middle of town, where they did a left turn at the convenience store, rode another half block, then he parked behind the police car in front of a small, square red brick building situated in the middle of two oak trees. The officer came back to Grant's car to escort him into the building. A few of Riverton's citizens gathered on the sidewalk next door and across the street, watching as the two men went into the police station.

The chief was sitting behind a desk. He stood up, smiled at Grant and motioned for the photographer to sit down. The chief remained standing. He wore the same color uniform as the cop who'd pulled Grant over, but the uniform fit better over his thin body, which was straight and taut, like a guitar's upper E string. His hair, thin and brownish-blond, was well-oiled, parted high on his right side and combed back. His face was like his body – narrow, and firm. He was clean-shaven, looked about 50 years old.

"Mind if I see your license and press card?" he said to the photographer.

Grant handed them over. Chief Hanson studied them for a couple of minutes, looking back and forth from the picture of Grant on his driver's license – a man with a clean-shaven face, unkempt, short brown hair and wire-rim glasses – to the man sitting in front of him – the same face, but perhaps a bit fatter, gray streaks in the hair, the same glasses.

"Guess that's you all right," the chief said. He grinned, showing Grant a row of straight, clean, evenly dispersed teeth. "Now the only question is why you've been taking all these pictures around town. Officer Gaines here tells me that you refused to answer his questions."

Grant offered the chief no explanation for the pictures, for his presence in the village of Riverton.

"You're not legally bound to talk to us, Mr. Baker," the chief said. "But the fact that you don't raises suspicions. You can understand that, what with what's going on in the world today, terrorism and bombings and such."

Grant stared at the chief, at his neat and clean appearance, at his efficiency in protecting the village from photographers.

"We have you for running a stop sign, for trespassing on village property, for harassing village residents, and we can add a couple of counts of failure to cooperate with an arresting officer. Or we can give you a ticket for running a stop sign – a $25 fine, Mr. Baker – and forget all the rest, if you'll just cooperate. Are these pictures for some kind of story you're doing for the Bulletin?"

Grant did not answer.

The police chief sighed. "Excuse us for a moment, Mr. Baker. Sal, come into the back with me."

Grant watched as the police chief and the arresting officer went into the next room, the thin, rigid chief followed by the cop and his flabby, wide butt that stretched the back seam of his pants.

Chief Hanson pushed the door shut. "Whadya think?"

"You got me, Fred. I don't understand why he's being so uncooperative."

"He didn't say one word to you?"

Sal shook his head and took out a cigarette. He tamped it on the back of his hand, then lit it with a silver Zippo he fished out of his pocket.

"I wonder what the Bulletin's up to," the chief said. "Remember that piece they did a few years ago, about small-town cops?"

"No."

"Yeah. Maybe it was before you came on. They didn't come here, but they did a story, interviews with police chiefs of small towns around here about the kinds of crimes they see the most, how they deal with 'em. You know, I think they call it human interest stuff. But I gotta tell ya, some of those cops they did came off lookin' pretty bad. But if that's what they're doing here, then wouldn't he at least talk to me?"

"You'd think so, Fred."

"Peek out there, see what he's doing."

"He'll see me peekin' if I open the door."

"Oh shit. Hold on."

The chief opened the door, went to his desk and grabbed a file folder from the upper right drawer. "Be right with you, Mr. Baker."

The chief started back for the door, then suddenly whirled around and faced the photographer. "How long you been with the Bulletin?"

Grant did not reply.

The chief turned again and disappeared behind the door.

"What was he doing?"

"Sitting there."

"What are we going to do?"

The chief tugged at his chin. He watched Sal blow a long, thick ribbon of smoke toward the ceiling.

"You give him his rights?" the chief finally said.

"Why should I? I didn't arrest him."

"Whadya mean you didn't arrest him? You

brought him in, didn't you?"

"He came voluntarily."

"Technically, Sal, he's under arrest. Now did you give him his rights?"

"Hell no."

"Geezuz. Hold on."

Chief Hanson went back through the door.

"Mr. Baker," he said. "I must warn you that anything you say may be used against you. You have the right to remain silent. You have the right to have an attorney present during questioning."

Grant listened to the chief.

"Excuse me," the chief said. He returned to the next room, shutting the door behind him.

"That's about all they could get us on," he said to Sal. "So far."

"What are you talking about?"

"Don't you understand what's going on here?"

Sal shook his head.

"They're doing another small-town cops kind of story. This time, they want to find out if we know what the hell we're doing. You know, things like reading a guy his rights, if we mistreat him when we bring him in, that kind of stuff. He's practically inviting abuse, the way he's refusing to answer our questions. And he doesn't have to. He knows his rights. Get it? He's using his right to remain silent and seeing if that will provoke us to take some kind of illegal action. It's a sting on small-town police forces."

"You think so?" Sal stuffed his cigarette into the tin ash tray on the empty desk.

"I know so."

"So what do we do?"

The chief grinned. "Nothing. Absolutely nothing."

"Fred, at the least, he ran a stop sign."

"People run stop signs all the time Sal. If we're not there and don't catch them, then technically, they didn't run it."

"Huh? But I did see him. I wrote up the ticket."

"Tear it up."

"Huh?"

"Don't you get it Sal? They would at least expect to be written up for something, just by the fact of being strangers in town doing strange things, like taking all those pictures. The fact that we write them up for a minor traffic ticket could be seen as harassment, even a minor form of it. Tear it up."

"OK. Then what?"

"Then we send him on his way. With a smile. No goddam big-city newspaper is going to make me or Riverton look stupid. Let them go up the road to Lakeside. C'mon. Let's get him out of here."

The two cops came through the door. Grant watched them approach, both of them stopping behind the desk.

"Mr. Baker," the chief said. "We have no idea what brought you to our village. But you're welcome here. Sal here says there's a good chance you might not have seen that stop sign, what with it being behind a tree and possibly obscured. Everybody who lives here, they know that stop sign's there. But you might not. No matter. We're going to forget this ticket. We want to extend you every courtesy and give you the benefit of the doubt."

Grant stared at the two men. He stood up. He started for the door, then stopped and looked at them again.

"No problem, Mr. Baker," Chief Hanson said. "I'm sorry if we've delayed you. Please, go about your business."

Grant went out of the building, glanced at the crowd of people gathered next door and across the street, about fifty of them, then climbed into his vehicle and drove back to where he'd left

Ralston.

He found the reporter sitting on the stoop of the house, writing in his notebook. Ralston stood up and came to the car, walking around to the driver's side. Grant scooted over.

"Where the hell you been?" Ralston said. "You get the plant?"

Grant shook his head no.

"Doesn't matter," Ralston said. "You can get it next time. We got another couple of families to interview, the cops and local officials. We'll be spending a lot of time in Riverton the next couple of days."

They turned around and drove back toward the middle of town. As they passed through the town's main intersection, they looked over and saw the crowd of residents at the police station.

"Must have caught someone speeding," Ralston said with a laugh, "or running a goddam stop sign. That's a big crime in this podunk town."

Grant saw the police chief and his officer step out of the station; the chief looked at Grant, their glances met, and the chief shot the photographer a quick grin before turning to explain the situation to the townsfolk.

"Looks like big doin's in Riverton," Ralston

said as they headed out of town.

V

Let us be silent that we may hear the whispers of the gods.

– Ralph Waldo Emerson

The massive dome of St. Peter's Church hung over Grant and Pauline, a heavenly umbrella of light green that descended to marble pillars and stained glass windows that were like intricate kaleidoscopes with their bright shards of red and blue and yellow and orange and purple. They depicted various stages of Jesus Christ's life – the carrying of the cross, the placing of the thorned crown, the hovering of angels above a manger; in each, the face of Jesus shone brightly, his blue eyes turned toward the dome of the church, his brown hair flowing freely to his shoulders, his beard and moustache full and radiant. At the front of the church, a statue of Jesus hung on a white cross in a recess behind the choir area and the organ.

A lone woman knelt a couple of pews back as she prayed silently.

Grant watched as Father Jessop emerged from a door to the right, walked to him and Pauline, stopped in the aisle, knelt and crossed himself as he faced the crucifix. Then he stood and looked at Grant and Pauline.

"Mr. and Mrs. Baker?"

They stood up. The priest smiled. "Follow me, please."

The three of them went through the doorway, into a small office. The priest pushed the door closed, then walked to the other side of a mahogany desk, motioning for Pauline and Grant to sit in the upholstered chairs that faced the desk.

"Welcome," he said, looking first at Grant, then at Pauline. "How can I help you?"

His voice was soft, friendly.

"Well, as I told you on the telephone, father, I'm, we're, just trying to find out why my husband has stopped talking."

The priest, wearing a pair of spectacles supported by thin, gold wire frames, nodded. His eyes flashed as the polished spectacles caught a ray of sunshine from the window that looked out onto a tree, where a robin sat on a branch and watched the three of them.

"I remember our conversation," he said.

"And you've been to the doctors."

Pauline nodded. "Medically, they can't find anything. He's continuing to see a psychiatrist. But, I just don't know."

The priest turned his head and studied Grant. Father Jessop wore a blue dress shirt over his white collar. His hair was white and swirled around his head in long strands like suds in a small whirlpool. His dark eyes shone behind his glasses. His lips were thin, set together and spread below a lean, long nose and a sharp, closely shaved chin. He had the face, the wrinkles, the wear, of a man in his sixties. He clasped his hands as though in prayer.

"Can you think of any distress, any at all, that he had been through?" the priest asked Pauline.

"Nothing. He went to work that morning, I left before he was up. I kissed him goodbye, he mumbled something about going out to dinner then went back to sleep. He usually sleeps about an hour later than me. Then when I came home that night – I'd stayed late at work for a faculty meeting – he was in the study listening to his music, silent as the night."

The priest looked again at Grant. "Anything unusual happen to you at work?"

Grant stared back.

"Nod if you can hear me."

"He can," Pauline said.

Grant nodded.

"Can you tell me if anything unusual happened at work that caused you to lose your ability to speak?" the priest said, still eyeing Grant. "Please, just nod."

Grant sat still.

Father Jessop looked back at Pauline. "How well does he communicate with you at home?"

"Well enough," she said. "I ask him yes and no kinds of questions; he usually responds. Or he shrugs his shoulders; he just recently started shrugging his shoulders. I see that as some small progress, actually. We communicate OK."

"What about when you talk about this problem?"

"Same response you just got," she said. "He doesn't want to, or can't, talk about whatever it is."

"What brought you to me?"

"I don't know. I'm a Catholic. Always have been. I don't know that you can do anything."

The priest nodded, his hands still clasped.

Pauline's voice cracked. "I guess I feel like

it has something to do with me. I mean, I talked to his boss. Everything was OK there. The doctor can't find anything. I thought things would get better for us after David got into college."

"Better?" the priest said. "What was wrong?"

"I don't know, but I guess something was. We didn't talk a lot. We didn't do a lot together. But that was how it's been for a long time. He had his job, his graduation and wedding pictures. I had my job. We had David. Grant and David didn't get along there at the last, before David went away to college. I figured it was a typical father-son kind of thing, you know. Sometimes he'd tell me that it didn't seem like we had much of a life together, that we didn't do anything together. But he talked less and less about that – about a lot of things, I guess. It's almost as if this silence is the natural culmination of a long period of declining talk between us."

"Had you fought before this happened?"

"Not really. I've talked to the psychiatrist about this. He seems to think it has something to do with sex, but I think our sexual relationship has been all right."

A tear rolled down Pauline's right cheek. Grant watched it, the tiny silver track it left from the corner of her eye to the middle of her cheek. Pauline wiped it away; both of her eyes glistened. She looked at Grant, then back at the priest.

"Did your fights ever turn violent?"

Pauline shook her head. "No. Mainly, he'd yell, I'd yell back, then he'd just go off and stop talking. You know, for a couple of hours or so, maybe all night. Once in awhile even a couple days. But never like this. Still, it must have something to do with me."

Father Jessop sighed. "I think you're jumping to conclusions. The guilt you're feeling is a natural reaction. Many times, when people face sudden change, a health crisis or financial setback, they take on feelings of guilt. They blame themselves. They think they deserve whatever has happened. They feel God is punishing them. But it doesn't work that way, Pauline. Usually, we punish ourselves far worse for a sin or a wrong that is far less significant than we think. Now, I'm no doctor or psychiatrist, but I just don't think whatever has caused this has anything to do with you. How long have you two been married?"

"Almost 25 years."

"Ever separated in that time?"

"No."

"Did the subject of divorce or separation

ever come up?"

"Nothing more than when he'd get mad, he'd say he wasn't going to keep putting up with it. But then he'd calm down and nothing more would be said."

"Did he ever make good on a threat, stay out maybe all night?"

"Once."

"Recently?"

She shook her head. "Maybe five years ago."

"No," the priest said, shaking his head slowly. "There's more to this than quarrels or marital strife, which seems to me to be pretty much normal. Everybody experiences what you two have. Sexual dissatisfaction, getting in a rut, general malaise. Those plague everybody."

Silence for a moment.

"I think he feels like he's failed in life," Pauline said.

"How so?"

"When he was younger, he always talked about quitting his full-time job and just doing photography, the kind of pictures he wanted to take. You know, he wanted to be an artist. Do documentary projects, artistic stuff. But there always seemed to be a reason not to. Our son. A house to pay off. Unexpected expenses. Now college. I kept telling him, the day will come, you can do your photography. Just be patient."

Pauline wiped away another tear. "I think maybe he's lost his patience with me, with life."

"I think maybe you and Grant have some issues to work out. I think maybe you and Grant need to find a common interest or two, a hobby, something you can do together."

The priest looked at Grant. "But there's never been anything stopping you from doing your photography. Artists, the great ones, have always managed to find the time and the place to do their art. Some did it full time, but many of them had other jobs they had to work to support their art. You know that, Mr. Baker."

He looked back at Pauline. "And you need to know that. It sounds to me like you two have a lot to talk about, that's all."

Pauline began to sob. "That's just it, father. We can't talk about things now."

The priest opened his upper right-hand drawer and took out a box of tissues. He pushed it across the desk to Pauline. She took out a couple and dabbed her eyes.

"I don't know, but I don't think this is a permanent condition," he said. "I think you will have an opportunity to talk things over. But conversations don't always require words between two people. You can talk, he can nod. You can come to understandings and agreements, can't you?"

"Yes," Pauline said, her voice quivering.

"Look," the priest said. "I don't know exactly what might be going on here. But you say Grant has his health. He's working, and doing fine at the job. You two do have a life, a child to get through college. There may never be any logical explanation for what's happened to Grant."

"But," the priest said, leaning back in his seat, "if we in the church relied on logic for explanation, we might well be out of business. We deal in faith, we deal in some things that can't be easily sensed, except by the heart, by what's inside. There is a plan for us, we do have a purpose to serve. Perhaps your husband has yet to serve his in a new or different way. There's no telling."

"You mean, there might be a reason for this?" Pauline said, crumpling the tissues in her hand. "There might be an unseen, unknown explanation?"

"I'm saying, sometimes we ask questions and seek answers that are there but are not ready to be revealed – but that may be revealed in time.

Or never at all. I'm saying, though, that there is a reason and a purpose for everything that happens. Just because we can't see or understand it doesn't mean it isn't there."

Pauline nodded.

"There is a biblical precedent for your husband's condition," the priest continued. "Zacharias, the father of John the Baptist, was struck dumb. He didn't believe it when an angel of God told him his wife would bear him a son – and his reason for doubting the news was pretty sound, as his wife had been barren and they both were getting on in years. Anyway, when he greeted the news of his coming fatherhood with skepticism, he lost his voice with the promise that it would be restored later, after his son was born."

"And was it?"

"Yes, after some disagreement over the name of the child, Zacharias got his voice back. Now, Pauline, I'm not suggesting that Grant is being punished by God or anything like that, understand. What I am suggesting, though, is that things sometimes happen mysteriously, things that we must simply accept on faith. For all we know, your husband's condition may be by choice – as men of religion and faith have taken vows of silence throughout history, as penance, as acts of worship, or as conditions of lifetime servitude."

Father Jessop leaned forward. He fixed his eyes on Pauline's, and he lowered his voice to a near whisper. "It may be, Pauline, that your husband has had a holy mark put upon him."

Pauline nodded her head slowly. "You mean, like a chosen one."

"Maybe," the priest said. He leaned back and resumed, in a normal tone. "Is Grant a religious man?"

"He hasn't been. He doesn't attend church, as you know."

"One needn't attend church to be a religious man."

"He's always told me that he doesn't believe," Pauline said.

The priest nodded. "Perhaps now he does. Perhaps now he does. Perhaps he always has, in his own way."

They both glanced at Grant, who was studying the robin that remained perched beyond the priest's window.

"As for your own doubts and questions, they are normal, Pauline," the priest said. "There, Zacharias serves as an example also. For a brief moment, he doubted the power of God. Now, Pauline, I'm not suggesting that you are somehow going to be punished for your own doubts. What I'm saying is that these doubts, these questions, your sense of guilt are all perfectly understandable. I don't believe God is a vengeful or punishing God; I believe the story of Zacharias is one of the Bible's many parables intended to underscore the importance of faith and acceptance. I think that is what you need right now, Pauline. Faith. And acceptance."

"Thank you, father. I understand. It's not easy, but I'll work on it."

"Matters of faith never are easy," Father Jessop said. "Jesus himself on the cross asked his father why he had forsaken him. You can be forgiven your questions."

Pauline stood up. She tapped Grant on the shoulder, urging him to stand also.

"Do you mind if I have a word alone with Grant?" the priest asked Pauline.

Pauline looked at the priest, then at Grant, then began backing toward the door. "No. Why?"

"Don't worry," the priest said. "I just want to talk to him."

"Okay." Pauline went out the door, closing it behind her.

Father Jessop clasped his hands together. He sighed, then fixed his gaze on Grant. Grant returned the gaze.

"Is there something you would like to tell me?" the priest said. He looked at the door, where Pauline had just left. "Anything you'd like to talk about, between you and me? I assure you, Grant, it would stay between you and me. I am duty bound to keep all such conversations private."

Grant continued to look at the priest. He watched the priest swallow, saw the slight pulse of the priest's heart beat at his throat, watched the priest's chest expand and contract as the priest breathed. Oxygen, blood, the lungs, the brain, the heart – these are life-sustaining, we accept the functions of these organs on faith, we take them and the life they sustain without questioning the principles, the reasons, behind them.

"You really are unable to speak, Grant?"

Grant watched and listened to the priest.

"I suspect, that in your own way, you are a man of faith and a man of belief," the priest said. "In fact, I know you to be a man of faith. You have faith that when you look through the lens of your camera, the picture you take will appear on paper much as you intended it to look. You have faith that people will look at your pictures and will understand what you intended to convey with them. But did you ever stop to think that people see other things in your pictures? That perhaps there is something in the background of one of them that you didn't notice but that somebody else sees? Or that perhaps some unintended lighting, a small nuance of focus, might shade your meaning so that the picture might be seen in a way other than that intended? As a photographer, Grant, you are a creator of sorts. Not only do you have faith that your camera will work and that your pictures will be viewed, you also have a hand in creating a world for those who view your work. You have faith in your ability to control and create that world – but that does not prevent those who see it from doubting or questioning what they see. Do you understand, Grant?"

Grant nodded. The priest grinned, pleased at being understood.

"Are you a man of faith, Grant?"

Grant nodded again.

"I am too, Grant," the priest said. "My faith is different than yours; my doubts the same as your wife's, though. We all have our own burdens that test our beliefs and our faith, Grant. Mine is a woman who learned last week she is dying of inoperable cancer. She is a lifelong member of the church, a woman raised on faith and on belief, a woman who continues her faith and belief in the face of death. Her faith is unshakable, Grant – but mine is not. She has come to me for strength, for counsel, for my services as conduit to God. I say the words to her, I pray with and for her. But when she leaves me, Grant, I ask God why. This woman has spent her life serving God. She has done countless charitable deeds. She has sacrificed her goals, her desires, and put those of others – her husband, her children, the needy – ahead of her own wants and needs. She has done this in the purest of spirit, not because of the rewards to be gained in an afterlife, not because of the righteousness she feels by her sacrifice, but because giving is who and what she is, it is her essence."

The priest sighed. He crossed himself, looked toward the door, where Pauline waited on the other side, then back at Grant.

"And yet God has chosen that this woman, who is my sister, must die – a fate she accepts without question, but one that I have been questioning daily. My sister, Mr. Baker."

The priest leaned forward. He peered into Grant's eyes; Grant felt the man's stare on his face, in his eyes.

"My sin, Grant, is that I am carrying a message that I sometimes do not believe. I wish right now that I had your affliction, that I could not say the words that I say to those who come through that door seeking my help – because I do not always believe the words I say. Oh, I accept them, on a certain level. I believe what I just told your wife to be true – that we must accept some things without question and with faith. I have been taught, and taught well, to believe that – by my parents, by my brothers, by those who came before me to this calling. But inside of me, in my soul, I am anguishing with doubts, with the possibility that I am representing a lie or a charade. This is blasphemy, Grant – or worse. I have confessed this sin to another, and I have been absolved – only to repeat the sin, and then again. My sister is dying, and I can do nothing for her but pray and give her a show of faith. A show, Grant."

The priest stood up. He went to the window, looked out at the branches of the tree, at the sky above it.

He turned back to Grant. "The worst sin of all is to repeat it knowingly. I envy you, Grant, because you are not a sinner. You don't believe in sin, therefore you don't sin. You live, you do the best you can, and for that you lose your voice. But you still have your faith in yourself and in your work, Grant. You have your faith in the love of your wife. I hope you're not feeling sorry for yourself, Grant, because you shouldn't. Your silence may be a great blessing; it certainly is no curse. Be grateful, Grant. That is the strongest prayer any of us can have. Gratitude. I don't even have that right now."

The priest sat down. Grant stood up. The priest looked up into Grant's face, gave Grant a slight smile. Then Grant turned and went through the door, closing it behind him.

"That took a while," Pauline said, rising from the dark, wooden pew where she had been waiting for her husband. She took Grant's hand and led him down the aisle, out the front doors of the church and into the sunshine, onto the firm sidewalk that split the cool, green lawn of the church, into the parking lot and their car.

In the front seat, Pauline reached out and laid her hand on Grant's knee. She patted his leg.

"I'm glad we came," she said. "It wasn't really confession, but I feel like I've just confessed. I hadn't really thought about this the way Father Jessop suggested – that maybe God has singled you out, that this is not so much a punishment as something else. Oh, I know you don't believe any of that stuff, Grant. But I do. Maybe someday you will too."

Pauline started the engine of the car, shifted into drive and took Grant home. He watched out the window, looking into the side-view mirror, saw the church grow smaller as they drove away, then disappear from view as Pauline turned the corner.

VI

No, my soul is not asleep.
It is awake, wide awake.
It neither sleeps nor dreams, but watches,
Its eyes wide open
Far off things, and listens
At the shores of the great silence.

– Antonio Machado

Grant lay on his back in the dark bedroom. A breeze blew across him from the window on his right; the white glow of the street light shone through the screen, landing on the wooden cedar chest beneath the window, laying down a soft layer of mottled light. Voices, an occasional cackle, came from the front porch across the street, where a beer party was in progress.

Long ago, Grant had gone to these parties, a young newspaper photographer, the next morning's paper put to bed at midnight. The parties always began at a downtown bar – this was when newspapers still had offices downtown and hadn't fled to the cheaper land tracts of the suburbs. Reporters, copy editors, photographers, all gathered at the bar, where they discussed that day's stories, the politicians whose lies and corruption would be exposed by upcoming editions, remembrances of politicians who had lost, who had survived, glories past.

Grant had begun straight out of journalism school at a small newspaper on the Montana prairie. The newspaper could not afford a full-time photographer; but he had taken some news-writing and editing courses. Grant sold himself as a photojournalist – as a reporter who carried his own camera and therefore could offer the newspaper two skills for the price of one. He covered city council meetings, county commission meetings, school board meetings and football games. It was a photo of a football game that helped Grant exit the small Montana town, where the wind blew incessantly in the winter, piling the snow into five- and ten-foot banks along the highway into and out of town, stranding motorists at the motel on New Year's Eve – Grant took his camera to the motel, where the band continued playing past 2 a.m.; the bar sold out of beer and the manager offered free coffee; truckers and dancers and stranded travelers filled all the beds and spilled out into the hallways for a night's sleep before the morning thaw. He took pictures of them all and produced a page 1 photo of a young man and woman, who had been strangers when they arrived at the motel, curled up in a lobby chair, covered with a blanket, and they left the place engaged to be married.

But it was Grant's photo of a game-winning field goal during a mid-season blizzard that got him out of that frigid town; he'd set up his tripod on the other side of the goal post, and he used a zoom lens to focus on the face of the kicker. Just as the kicker was following through, the football leaving his right toes, Grant shot, capturing the kicker's grimace, his wide eyes behind the cross bar of the football helmet, the brown football just rising from his toe to begin its game-winning journey between the crossbars, the glow of the stadium lights shining in the background. The photo was picked up statewide by the Associated Press, then it moved on the national wires, leading to a telephone call from a photo editor at a city newspaper in Colorado. Six months of Montana dues paid off for Grant, who packed his bags into the trunk of his car, stayed for one last late night of beers paid for by the managing editor, the newspaper's three full-time reporters and the composing foreman, who took Grant to his

Lion's club after the bar closed, and the reporters, composing foreman and Grant played table shuffleboard until 4 a.m., when they broke for coffee and pancakes at the truck stop five miles out of town and Grant hit the road, driving south – in time for spring.

Grant felt the breeze blow across his chest, listened to Pauline's soft snore as she lay on her left side, her back to him. He listened to the party, which had quieted to voices chatting on the porch across the street, an occasional beer popping. Among the whir of the crickets singing their night song, he could hear the click of a cigarette lighter being shut, a quick burst of laughter from a woman, followed by a whoop.

He met Pauline in Colorado when he showed up at the local elementary school to shoot a photo essay of children enjoying a performance by a traveling acting troupe. She too was in the beginning of her career. He told her of his plans – to work a few years as a newspaper photographer and shooting more artistic stuff on the side, which he hoped to one day display in a gallery. She joined him for some of the after-work drinking sessions, listened to the stories and the exploits, to the pleasures the writers and editors took in exposing corruption, destroying careers, baring hypocrisy.

"Don't you ever get a kick out of making someone look good in the paper?" she asked him once.

The response, a look that made her feel like an invader from another universe, taught her the basic journalistic philosophy – the credo that nobody is in the business for the money; rather, they do it for the opportunity to fix the world, or, as they got older, to at least mend their small corner of it. Or they're in it until something with more money comes along, usually public relations – what committed journalists called the dark side, in which writers and photographers trade their ethics and their souls for the lies and the dollars of public relations. Or they simply like writing and taking pictures and dealing with the powerful, the famous, the rich – and with just plain people who are living their lives under similar, honorable codes.

"It's the only honorable profession," a drunken wire editor told Pauline one night, one of the last nights she joined the newspaper people in their Friday night gatherings.

"What about law?" she asked in response.

"Please. Don't use the word lawyers and honorable in the same sentence," came the reply.

"Teaching?"

The table quieted. All present looked at Pauline the teacher.

"OK," the editor allowed. "There are two honorable professions in the world."

Pauline smiled.

"But only one that lets you put the screws to the assholes of the world."

Glasses went up all around, beer poured down throats.

"Don't you think any professions have honest people left?" Pauline asked the boothful of drinkers, who had also claimed a couple of neighboring tables, a pinball game and a shuffleboard table.

"I don't know," one reporter yelped from a pool table. "What do I look like, Diogenes?"

Laughter all around, along with more drinks.

"I'm sorry," Pauline said. "But I believe there are honest lawyers, honest politicians, honest salesmen – even honest reporters."

She smiled at the gang, her eyes landing on Grant.

That was the night that Grant knew he loved Pauline and that he wanted to take her home – away from all this – and to stick her in a safe place, like you do with a rare jewel, where nobody but he could enjoy her.

Grant sat up in bed, craned his neck toward the window, trying to hear what the across-the-street neighbors were talking about. He heard occasional words, mixed in with laughter ... "goddam asshole ... owe too much money ... big titties ... hand over a beer ... fuckin' eat shit ... me now, my turn ..."

Party talk.

He looked down at Pauline, at the side of her body as it moved up and down with her breathing. She slept with her knees bent. He reached out and touched the arc of her hip, ran his hand along it like you gently rub the fine wood of a polished old stair railing.

"Mmmff," Pauline said.

From Colorado, they moved to New Mexico, Texas, Oklahoma, Pennsylvania, Ohio. His career had taken them across the country. They'd seen big cities at night, listened to jazz and drunk white and red wine to wash down shrimp scampi and oysters in jazz clubs, taken summer walks along tree-shaded sidewalks, visited art museums and galleries, taken David to aquariums, planetariums and museums of natural history, slept in Rocky Mountain lodges, picnicked with their son, watched him play ball, perform music, recite poetry, ride bicycles, dye hair, pierce ears, drive cars, throw up booze, march for graduation, pack up and move away to college.

Grant had taken pictures of it all. Photos, boxes and files of negatives, all documenting his work, his career, his and Pauline's life together.

Lying back in his bed, with a front-porch beer and cigarette party going across the street – the breeze carried a faint aroma of burning tobacco into the room – and his wife dozing next to him, Grant flipped through the photographs in his memory.

The standoff in Tulsa, when a robber holed up in a high-rise bank, Grant went to the building across the street, marched into an office, flashed his press badge, and he camped at an open window, focusing his camera on the bank, locating the robber at a window, where he spoke with police on the telephone while holding office workers prisoner. Grant used three rolls of film, one frame of which made the next morning's front page, a zoom shot of a blurry man holding a gun in one hand and a telephone in the other, beneath the headline: Gunman Surrenders. There was a front page photo of lake divers in Ohio as they pulled out the body of a drowned teenager who'd toppled off a speedboat, the photo captured the shadowy ripples of the gray water that moved away from the divers' boat like wet sound waves pulsating through the sky; an investigation found the kid had consumed a six-pack of beer before getting on the boat and had drunk two more while on the boat. The boat owner was charged and convicted of negligent homicide. There were a couple of page one photos of cops in gas masks and helmets confronting a group of rioters, the air thick with gas that hovered in the photo like a thin mist as the camera captured a billy club smashing the skull of a bearded, bespeckled, unarmed rioter, the companion photo depicting the mayor angrily shouting down a group of protesters that had converged on city hall demanding an end to the police siege of the neighborhood of the riots – all prize-winning photographs of breaking news. There were nature pictures: a monarch butterfly that had landed on the nose of an Irish Setter in a sunny, grass-strewn city park; purple irises in full bloom surrounded by lush, green ivy climbing a red brick wall at a city university; a deer rubbing its antlers against the bark of a tree, taken in early morning so that the sun shone on the deer's face and cast the crevices and crannies of the tree into dark shadows that contrasted with the bright sun-lit images of the deer, with the shedding, dangling skin of the antlers, and tree – all photos that had won Grant and his newspapers awards for feature photography. Grant remembered some of the students he had photographed for their graduation and yearbook photos: the kid who had covered his face with makeup to try to hide the scourge of his acne, whose father paid for the photographs and then paid more money for a studio touchup job so the world would never see, in print, his son's scarred face; the girl in the wheelchair, a straight-A student who could not walk because of muscular dystrophy, who smiled proudly into the camera, her brown eyes sparkling behind black frame glasses, her teeth white and straight and framed by straight black hair that was cut in an even bowl around her head; one girl had Grant shoot her in the woods, where she posed leaning against the trunk of a pine tree, sitting among a clump of wildflowers, and when the shoot was nearly done, she asked Grant to take a couple of extra poses, which she would pay for separately, for her boyfriend, and after Grant agreed, she removed her blouse and bra, then her skirt and panties, shoes and socks, and she again leaned against the tree, staring into the camera with her bright blue eyes and clean brown hair with a come-on look that flushed Grant's face as he focused on the yellow and blue butterfly tattoo near the top of her left breast.

Lying awake in bed, Grant remembered the pictures of his career, the football games, the speeches, the playground scenes, the fires, the shootings, the sirens, the car crashes, the bodies – so many bodies, so much blood and death.

Grant sat up abruptly. He noticed the silence. The noise that had filled his window – the porch party, the crickets, the breeze – had stopped. His wife, still on her side, breathed quietly. He threw back the sheet, got out of bed and walked around the end of the bed, out the door, down the hallway and into the bathroom. He turned on the light – Pauline had always wondered why he needed the light to urinate in the middle of the night – and, after flushing, he stood in front of the mirror above the sink. He studied his head, his face, his upper body. His hair, half gray now, was barely mussed; he'd cut it about an inch short five years ago and kept it that way so that when he got out of the shower, all he had to do was dry it and let it go where it would. His face was ready for a shave, erratic silver and brown whisker stubbles sprouted on his chin, his lower cheeks, above his lips, which had remained muscular and thick since his trombone days in high school. Grant's neck was thin, his skull oblong, egg-like. He remembered the face of the boy who had stared back at him so long ago; the change had been so gradual and complete over the years that the boy who used to be in the mirror seemed now like someone else – not someone he regretted losing so much as someone who simply was no more, who had evolved into the Grant that stared back at him now – a man in middle age, whose face had begun to wrinkle, whose eyes had lost their dark brown hue and were now brownish-green. Grant tried to take an objective look at the face, the skull – at the mechanics behind and inside the face and skull, the blood that rushed to and from his head, the air that went into the mouth and nostrils and then came back out, re-cycled as carbon dioxide, the nerve cells that carried the messages from his brain to his body – all of it stored neatly in the neck, like wires buried in cable, between the skull and the body, all of it in the most vulnerable place of the body, unpro-tected. Deer and elk have antlers; tortoises have their shells; humans, though, have nothing but brittle, breakable bone to protect their brains, nothing but seven layers of skin to shield their necks – that is what separates them from glass, sharp edges, hard walls, the hazards that sur-round necks and heads, brains and blood, every day.

Grant swallowed; he watched his Adam's apple move as he swallowed, felt his mouth juices go down his throat. He reached over, switched off the bathroom light and stared for a moment at the sudden blackness in the mirror, then followed his route back down the hallway to the top of the stairs, where he turned and descended to the study. He switched on a lamp, searched through a stack of CDs until he found his John Coltrane Giant Steps album. He switched on the sound system, inserted the CD, adjusted the volume – low; Pauline had never appreciated his late-night jazz excursions in the study – and went to the easy chair opposite the matching bookcases.

Coltrane's "Naima" emerged from the speakers on top of the bookcases at each corner of the room. The tenorman's moody saxophone explored the sultry chords that he had written in tribute to his wife.

Grant listened to the breathy ballad as Coltrane played his sax, blowing his drug- and booze-ravaged soul, his love for his wife, into his golden tenor saxophone. The song wailed of a tremendous and tumultuous love, the love of an artist who became a believer and who preached his soul and seduced his lover in the notes of the song he had written for her.

Pauline entered the room, sat down in her chair, next to her husband. He looked at her, blinked his eyes. She stared back at him, a stare that became a glare.

"Why are you doing this?" Pauline's voice stabbed through Coltrane's sax. Her eyes were sad, pleading, questioning. "Why?"

Grant sat up straight, gazing at his wife, at the shadows that the lamp cast across her face and upper torso, at the dim features of her face.

"I don't know how much more of this I can take," Pauline said, her voice rising. "I don't understand why you can't write me a note explaining this to me. From the doctor I get nothing. The psychiatrist says not a whole lot is known about this thing but he thinks you'll come out of it someday, like you're in some kind of emotional coma or something. I don't understand, Grant. Is it me? What did I do? What did I do?"

Grant said nothing as Coltrane blew love notes to his wife.

"This isn't fair, what you're doing to me," Pauline said. She spoke clearly, her voice steady, but angry and loud. "I've moved across the country with you, leaving good teaching jobs and starting over and starting over. I've put up with your moods. It hasn't been easy, Grant, but I've been there all the way for you. Now you've just disappeared on me. I mean, I've got your body, I've got you; but I don't have you. I just can't believe that people stop talking for no reason. What the hell happened? What have I done?"

Grant stood up and went to his wife, softly grabbed hold of her arms, and he pulled her to her feet. He looked into her face, she looked back. Their eyes sparkled like clear marbles in the dim light of the room, reflecting the lamp's yellow bulb.

"Remember how sometimes, late at night, you'd put on some of your jazz and make me dance with you?" she said. "I never liked dancing, but you made me do it anyway. Dance with me now, Grant."

They held each other in an embrace and danced, a slow dance, into the living room, among the couch and coffee table and easy chair, across the soft carpet, both of them in bare feet, Grant in his underpants and T-shirt, Pauline in her knee-length sleeping shirt. Then the song was over; Coltrane's tender saxophone melody drifted off. Pauline went to the sound system, shut it down, and she took Grant by the hand, leading him up the stairs. They went to the bedroom; she gently pushed Grant onto the bed, then got in next to him, on top of the cool sheet with the window open next to them, the hazy streetlight and black sky visible beyond the screen. She lifted off her sleeping shirt, then reached down and pulled off his underpants. She lay on top of him and kissed his forehead, his cheeks, his mouth; she reached down between his legs and fondled him, felt him grow in her hand.

"You used to say I didn't like doing this," she said, softly now, into his ear. "You were so wrong."

She kissed him again. They embraced; she pulled Grant into her and she lay on top of him as they made love in the early morning, both of them panting, gasping, then heaving a long sigh as Grant finished and spread his arms out to his sides. Pauline stayed on top of him, her breasts pushing into his chest. He could feel her pulse in her body, could feel his own heart throbbing. He put his arms around her and clasped her to him. He kissed her neck. Then, she rolled off of him; the breeze blew across his damp chest, cooling him.

Pauline lay an arm across Grant's stomach and softly stroked his abdomen. Then she rested her arm gently across his thigh.

"How was that?" she said, then grinned. "No need to answer. You always liked it when I got on top, didn't you?"

Pauline leaned into her pillow. She sighed. "We're going to get through this, whatever it is," she said, nearly whispering. "I don't understand it; I don't know if you understand it, if you're afraid of it, if you maybe even are enjoying it. I've thought about this; I imagine it's nice sometimes not having to talk with people, just simply tuning them out and going about your own thoughts, your own business. Not having to respond to my ramblings. The thought has crossed my mind that you're deliberately doing this just because you're tired of people, of me, that this is just the best way you've found to deal with the world. But that would be OK too, Grant. I'm still here; I'm not going anywhere. I can still talk to you and I know you can hear and understand me. Only I'm talking less and less these days. Maybe that's good too. Maybe I'm learning that sometimes it's OK, sometimes it's even good, to be quiet, to listen instead of to talk – though I have to talk in my work, y'know? I'm a teacher. You can't do that without talking. You, you don't need to talk to take pictures. I guess you can say whatever it is you want to say with your camera – with your heart, maybe. Maybe this is the way for you to finally do what you've always said you wanted to do – just take pictures and to just be appreciated for that. Or maybe Father Jessop is right. Maybe God's touched you in a special way. I know you don't believe in God Grant; and I know you don't understand the God I believe in, though I've tried to explain it to you. But there's something there, Grant. Something that sustains life, that moves things in ways we can't see or understand."

Pauline softly stroked Grant's inner thigh.

"You know, I wake up when I hear you blink," she said. "We're connected. When you're awake, I'm awake. I know you're not sleeping a lot, at least at night. I know you're having dreams. I can feel you having them. So I'm not sleeping at night either. I'm awake with you. So we'll not sleep, and if necessary not talk, through life together."

Grant nodded in the darkness. Pauline felt his nod. She squeezed his thigh to let him know.

VII

I need to be alone. I need to ponder my shame and my despair in seclusion; I need the sunshine and the paving stones of the streets without companions, without conversation, face to face with myself, with only the music of my heart for company.

– Henry Miller, Tropic of Cancer

Grant watched Clevenger's Adam's apple move up and down the doctor's thin throat as Clevenger talked.

"I was raised to believe that sex was a sin, that it was a forbidden fruit," the doctor said. "I remember, when I was about seven years old, some kids up the block had a clubhouse they'd built in their backyard. I was up there playing with one of their little brothers one day; they invited us into the club. The older boys were nine, ten; there were the two of them, and me and Danny. We thought we were hot shit, being invited into the older guys' clubhouse. They had a girlie magazine in there, you know, not like Playboy or Penthouse, but something raunchier with full frontal nudity. They showed us the pictures in it; God, I remember the tremendous sense of guilt I felt looking at those pictures, at those naked breasts and the naked crotch. The women stood there for the camera, undressed, and I tell you, I felt a movement in my pants. And the older boys knew this. They made me and Danny pull our pants down, and we stood there in front of them, our little penises hard and hairless; they started laughing. Man, I pulled my pants up, and quicker than they knew what happened, I was out of there and running home. I left Danny behind; I heard them laughing, guffawing, as I ran down the sidewalk to my house. I ran into our kitchen, my face red, my eyes puffy, bawling to my mother. She sat me down at the kitchen table, and she listened to my whole story. Well, I knew just a few sentences into it that I'd made a mistake. Boy, her eyes grew bigger and her face redder as I told her what those boys had shown us and what they'd done to us. I finished my story; she grabbed me by the hand and took me out back, where she cut a switch from an elm tree, pulled my pants down and she whipped my bare bottom until she raised red welts. And when my father came home, she talked to him and they grounded me for a week."

The doctor sighed and folded his hands

on his desk. "So I learned a lot that day that I got my pants taken down two times by people older and stronger than me. I learned never to tell my mother anything that happened to me sexually, even if it wasn't my fault, because in her eyes any sexual occurrence was a sin and had to be beat out of the sinner. I learned never to tell on the other kids, because my mother called up their parents and let them have it. I was ostracized in that neighborhood for a long time, until they finally needed a kid to play outfield at a pickup game – but I never saw the inside of that clubhouse for a long time, until much later in my life, when Danny and I went there to smoke and to drink. And I learned about how powerful guilt can be, because that emotion stayed with me a lot longer than the welts on my behind. It stayed with me through two marriages, at least, in which I was sexually inhibited, in which I took every opportunity to seek out extramarital affairs where I could carry out my fantasies that my wives – and of course, my mother, because I don't think my father would have made a big deal out of this episode were it not for her – did not approve of. I finally erased those guilt feelings; today I see sex for what it is. But it took a lot of study on my part, a lot of humiliation, even some counseling."

The doctor nodded at Grant, as though reading his mind. "Yes, Grant, even psychiatrists go for counseling and therapy. We need it just as much as any other human being."

The two watched each other for a moment.

"Years later, when I was involved in my studies at the university, I came to realize that had I been a seven-year-old boy in Europe instead of America, what happened to me likely would have been considered nothing more than an initiation. Had my parents been European instead of American, they likely would have talked to me about what happened in that clubhouse, they might have used the situation to teach me something about sex, about masturbation, about the male body, that the penis is intended for sexual pleasure and procreation and is not the object or subject of humiliation or guilt. But I am an American, Grant. And in America, despite all of its sexual liberation, sexual activity remains sinful and dirty – at least, so far as children are concerned."

The doctor leaned forward, keeping his hands clasped so that from Grant's viewpoint, the doctor's Adam's apple was a bouncing ball above the joined fists. "Don't misunderstand, Grant. I'm not saying America is bad. I'm simply saying that this country's sexual mores and attitudes are out of whack with the rest of the world. We're the most sexually repressed nation of the industrialized countries. We feel guilt more than any other nationality over the sexual act. And thus, we're more obsessed with sex, its organs, its purpose and its complex behaviors than are any other people."

Clevenger looked at his watch. "And our hour's about up."

He glanced up at Grant. "I feel that we're making progress, Grant," he said. "I sense a communication between us; I sense that you are taking in what I say, that you take it home and digest it. I think it would be to your benefit to continue these sessions for awhile, and I'll have Betty make the arrangements."

Grant stood up and turned to leave.

"Oh, by the way," the doctor said.

Grant stopped, turned around.

"I've gotten in touch with a colleague whose done some research on the subject of selective mutism. He's on the west coast, but he's been working on a case of which he's made a study and is preparing a paper. His subject is a middle-aged man; these are rare with this disorder. Most cases involve children and are less pronounced.

But this man's subject suffers symptoms highly similar to yours; we're wondering if there might be a possibility for an internet support group if we can find even a couple more."

The doctor chuckled. "Of course, that's liable to be a rather non-communicative support group, isn't it? But you never know; perhaps down the road there is a possibility for dialogue; this doctor shares my opinion that the disorder can be overcome, over time. Nonetheless, he and I are in communication, and I thought you might like to know you are not alone."

The doctor nodded to Grant, dismissing him from the office. "We'll see you same time next week then, eh?"

Grant turned and walked out the door. He stopped at the receptionist's desk, where Betty gave him a card with a time and date of the next appointment written on it. Grant proceeded to the parking lot where he got in his car and drove back to work.

The afternoon budget meeting was going on in the conference room, behind its glass partitions that looked out onto the newsroom, when Grant walked into the office at about 4:30 p.m. The whole complex was glass – tall, thick, tinted windows overlooking the rolling hills of the landscaped 10-acre newspaper park complex north of the city; glass partitions setting aside the main newsroom, which was wide open, from the offices of the editors – whom the subeditors, reporters and photographers called glassholes, and not affectionately.

Grant found a note from Walt in his box.

"Stick around till after the budget meeting. Fisher wants to talk to us."

Grant sat down at Walt's desk and gazed toward the conference room, where Fisher sat at the head of the long, mahogany table, with the various editors seated on either side. He counted the editors: eight of them, all in white shirts and neckties except one female, who wore a blue blouse and black slacks and a pair of shining thick black hoops that dangled from her ears like a pair of tire swings from a tree covered in stringy, hanging black leaves.

The city editor, Don Brackman, was talking.

"We got lucky on this one, Derek," Brackman said, his brown frame glasses halfway down his nose, his eyes peering over them at the newspaper editor. "Ralston got the call just before he was leaving to go out on an interview. It was a friend of his in Customs."

"How many busted?"

"They got between 25 and 30 illegals working just at the Bingham Farms plant, not counting field workers, but Ralston hasn't gotten an official count yet. He's up there now with Tracy."

"Federal charges?"

"Yeah. And the state's come in on it too."

Brackman chuckled.

"What's funny?" the editor said.

"Oh, the sheriff. He called us up about an hour ago to tip us on this – like he didn't know we were already onto it. I think he just this afternoon found out about the biggest illegal alien bust in his county in the past decade, at least."

Fisher nodded. "Yeah. Which reminds me, we'll need a history of the company, any previous busts, and we'll want to get some numbers from the feds – you know, what's the previous biggest illegal alien bust in the nation, that kind of stuff, for a box to go with Ralston's story."

"Can do," Brackman said.

"That all?" Fisher said.

"Other than the continuing strike out at the foundry."

"Take that one inside," Fisher said. "What's big on the wire?"

"Surprise, surprise," said Benjamin Lance,

the wire editor. He sat at the end of the table, on the editor's left, in his white shirt and black bow tie. "Another raid on the West Bank, five more dead, one more ultimatum from the Israelis."

"Gimme somethin' new, would ya?" Fisher said. "I'm tired of the Middle East. Can't the wires find us a good sex scandal in Congress or the White House? Have all of our national leaders stopped fucking their pages and interns, or what?"

Lance shrugged his shoulders and clamped down on his unlit pipe, which he sucked on all night like a baby's pacifier, until the front page went back to the shop and he stepped outside and leaned against the brick facade between the entryway and the window to at last have a long, luxuriant smoke.

So it went, around the table, each editor feeding his or her best story to Fisher for consideration for the front page. From sports, the university had narrowed its list for a new men's basketball coach to two finalists – based on unofficial sources.

"Out front," Fisher said. "I love it when we find out stuff those university assholes are sitting on. We'll shove this one up their asses – but down-page. It isn't official yet."

From features, the symphony musicians were threatening to strike next season if they didn't get better health benefits.

"It's not about money," assistant managing editor for features/business Angela Hopp said. "They say they can't afford to pay their own premiums any more and want the symphony to pay it all."

"Bullshit it's not about money. Same old sad tune," Fisher said. He grinned at his musical pun. "Take it on the features cover, but keep an eye on this story. You know how that goddam Metro rag likes to beat us on the artsy-fartsy stuff."

Ralston's story on the illegal alien bust at Bingham Farms was the day's top story and would go above the fold, with a photo of an illegal being led away in handcuffs and a mug shot of the company CEO, who after the bust immediately held a press conference announcing an internal crackdown on the company's hiring practices. The basketball coach story would go in a single column, also above the fold. The Middle East, a feature story on American eating habits and the national obesity problem and a late-afternoon stock market dive would finish out the front page.

Fisher asked Walt and Brackman to stay

behind as the other editors filed out of the room to begin work on filling out the next morning's remaining news pages.

"We're going to have to bump up Ralston's series on the migrant workers," Fisher said. "I don't want to sit on it now that we have a hard news peg on it. This illegal bust ties right in to what his series is all about."

"How soon?" Brackman said.

"Week from Sunday? The alien bust story ought to stay alive at least that long."

Brackman nodded. The sun shone through the window that looked onto the court-yard beyond the conference room, highlighting the city editor's freckled face, his reddish-blonde hair that was beginning to thin at the top.

"Let's look at the pictures," Fisher said.

Walt took the computer printouts from a file folder and shoved the stack of photos to Fisher. The editor thumbed through them for about five minutes, nodding his head. He lifted a couple, held them up and studied them, then put them in a separate pile.

"Good stuff," he said.

"Goddam right," Walt said. "Excellent stuff."

Fisher nodded. "I think this one, shot

THE SILENT TREATMENT

from a distance, showing the whole village – it's the lead art. Look at it."

Fisher handed the photo to Brackman, who eyed it for about a minute.

"What do you see in that?" Fisher said.

"I see elements of the entire series," Brackman said. "I mean, Ralston's got it all. He's got village officials talking about the impact of the turkey operation on their economy, he's got sociologists and professors talking about the lives and lifestyles of the migrant community. This photo is what it's all about."

"Lead photo?" Fisher said.

"Absolutely."

"You agree?" Fisher looked at Walt.

"Yep," Walt said. He grinned. "I liked this one from the beginning."

Fisher thumbed through the photos some more – pictures of villagers involved in family and community activities; migrant children in the classroom; portraits of fathers, mothers, sons, daughters; photographs of the village Catholic priest, social workers interacting with children and families; village and county officials at work.

Fisher shook his head. "Goddam, Walt. Your boy did all right on these."

Walt grinned, his teeth flashing beneath

his moustache, and nodded.

"Lookit this one," Fisher said, dealing a portrait of a mother suckling a child to Brackman. "What do you see there?"

The photo was in black and white, the woman's face in half light and half shadow, her complexion like soft ivory, her hair black and in a long braid hanging from the back of her head. The child's hair was a fuzzy black smudge on top of a pale face with fat cheeks. The mother's breast was in shadow.

"Pathos," Brackman said without hesitation. "That's what this series is all about – about the plight of these people. Man, this could have been the cover photo for Grapes of Wrath. These are the people who are victimized by the plant, by the government, by the U.S. economic system."

Fisher nodded. "Walt?"

"I think this picture is about hope," the chief photographer said. "Now, I haven't read the series, so Brackman knows more what he's talking about there. But I look at this, I see this as symbolizing the future of these people – a future that lies with government policy and plant decisions – decisions that feed or starve these people."

Fisher nodded again. "I see a goddam good photo. It's about the love of a mother for her child, that's all. Amid all the strife and labor and politics and these people's hard life, they're no different than any other mother and child in any society. That's what this picture says."

"I guess it says a lot of things," Walt said.

Fisher shot Walt a glance.

"It's a damn fine photo," Brackman said. "To go with a damn fine interview he's got with that woman – along with some other folks he interviewed."

Fisher pushed the pile of photos back to Walt. "You guys go over these and match them with the stories – but leave out some good ones. I think I just found our next lobby photo display. We'll put these out in the lobby the Sunday we begin the series, and we'll have a reception that afternoon. Goddam, from what I've seen of the writing so far, and now these photos, we got one hell of a package coming up."

Fisher stood up. Walt and Brackman started for the door.

Walt stopped and faced Fisher.

"You still want to see me and Baker?"

"Yeah," Fisher said. "For a minute or two."

"I saw him come in earlier. I'll bring him to your office," Walt said.

Moments later, Walt and Grant walked

into the editor's office.

"Close the door and have a seat," Fisher said, sitting at his desk. From his vantage point, he could look beyond the two photographers and see the newsroom, the reporters at their desks, typing into their computers, editors peering over reporters' shoulders at story leads or reading stories on their computers. Walt and Grant looked past Fisher, out the window, onto a vast lawn, where a rotating sprinkler dusted the vast greenery.

"Baker, I just looked over your work on the migrant series. Good stuff." The editor stood, walked to the window, then turned and smiled at the photographer.

Grant watched the smile appear, like an upside-down V. Fisher's entire demeanor was a big V, from the narrow, white widow's peak that began at a point just at the junction of his pale forehead and his bushy white eyebrows and then spread backwards, widening to fill in his head down to the ears. Below that, Fisher's chin began at a point just above his neck, and then his skull followed the same V pattern to its wide dome above a face accented by dark slashes of eyes set in milky skin that pinkened when the editor was excited or angered. And then again, his broad shoulders narrowed to a thin waist, below which wide hips tapered to pointy black shoes that were polished to a sheen that matched the gleam of the editor's hair.

Derek Fisher looked like no other man, a svelte, aerodynamic, triangular walking piece of Picasso cubism, perfectly symmetrical, spreading upward and outward like a human formation of geese flying south.

"But I kind of wonder what's going on with the rest of your work," Fisher continued. He stopped, studying Grant's face for a reaction. There was none.

"I had to send Tracy out with Ralston today on a story out at the Bingham Farms," Fisher said. "The feds busted the place for harboring illegal aliens. It's a huge story, Baker. Then I found out that you were out there the other day with Ralston for his series, and you were supposed to go out to the plant and take some pictures there. Only you never showed."

The editor stopped again, waiting for a reaction from the photographer. What he got was a shuffle in the seat next to Grant, where Walt uncrossed and then recrossed his legs.

"We got a photo, but you should have been here today to take it," Fisher continued. "We had to take Tracy off of some studio work she was doing for next week's food page; you were out on a doctor's appointment."

"Psychiatrist," Walt said. He opened his mouth to say more, but Fisher looked at him with his black, V-shaped eyes, and Walt closed his mouth.

"Now I know you're having some kind of problem," Fisher said, looking again at Grant. "But you need to schedule your doctors' appointments for non-working hours. We needed you here today. Fact is, we should have already had some file photos of people working at that turkey plant. Chances are one of them would have been an illegal. But even if that weren't the case, we're going to have to send you back out there to shoot the plant and what goes on there to go with the series, which we've decided to move up. It's going a week from Sunday."

Fisher turned his gaze again to Walt. "I'll leave it to you two to make whatever arrangements have to be made. Ralston's going to be busy finishing up his interviews and writing."

Fisher sat quietly for a moment, then narrowed his eyes, dark slits on pinkish skin.

"Then there was that goddam auto accident you shot just before you took your sick leave," Fisher said. "You came in here and left us with a picture of a car smashed into a tree. That was it. A car smashed into a tree. TV had cops and ambulances. The other newspapers in the region had the corpse being carried out. We had a smashed car. Now I don't know what the hell's going on with you, Baker. But it stops now. Sickness is fine; it's excusable. But missing assignments is not and won't be excused. That's it. I don't want any more blown assignments or you'll be back here again, and it will be less gentle."

The three of them sat quietly for a moment, the door closed, the office a silent, glass cocoon while telephones rang and computer keys clicked in the newsroom and the water sprinkler hissed and sprayed outside. Grant stared at the editor's face, at the contrasting blacks and whites and reds, the colors of the old newspaper joke. It was a rigid, clean face, one that could have been drawn on white paper in charcoal its features were so distinct and clear.

"I don't think we'll be having this conversation again," Fisher said. He smiled and stood up. Walt stood up, then Grant.

Walt led Grant back to the photo department, then to his desk. They sat down.

"I swear, brother, I didn't see that one

coming."

Grant looked at Walt, at his round, easy face, his wide eyes, his red nose. Grant had never given much attention to people's faces, not until his voice went away. He found that, like people who lose their vision learn to rely more on their other senses, he had a heightened awareness not only of faces, but of voices, conversation, the look of the world and the people in it. He was paid, as a photographer, to pay attention to the visuals of the world; but he never had quite so keenly observed them before.

"Don't worry about it," Walt said. "Why don't you get out of here and go home to Pauline. I think he's just in a mood. This migrant series has him on edge. Just make sure you show up for your assignments and then shoot them, that's all. You'll be OK."

Grant had heard a lot of people telling him recently that he would be OK.

VIII

Quiet is peace. Tranquility. Quiet is turning down the volume knob on life. Silence is pushing the off button. Shutting it down. All of it.

– Khaled Hosseini, The Kite Runner

Grant was heading back into town from a morning of shooting the turkey plant in Riverton and could see the dark clouds boiling over the city, its taller buildings poking up into the swirling atmospheric muck. He listened to the police radio in his car as he drove toward town. Squad cars were being called out for fender benders. Then he saw it, the tumultuous dark storm on the outskirts of the city, just as he heard the report on the radio that a twister had been spotted.

He watched as the storm moved over the city. On either side of him, dust blew, carrying leaves with it; birds twittered in the air like they do, helter-skelter, when the wind is strong and erratic.

Traffic had begun to slow. Suspecting an accident or a jam from a downed tree, he turned off the highway onto a county road that headed east, toward the worst of the storm. He'd been over these roads numerous times and knew the short cuts, the direct routes, the alternative ways to reach the high schools, the village centers, the obscure streets, the dead ends, the businesses – all places where he had chronicled the community life, its sorrows, its triumphs, over the past decade.

Grant had come to care about this community the way one cares about a place that is home – he despised those who would wrong it; he admired those who worked to make it better; he despaired in its tragedies, rued its faults, cheered its victories. Now, he knew the part of town where the storm was most intense, a transition zone from suburban neighborhoods to industrial parks to farm and grazing land.

A tree branch skipped across the road and then soared into the air with other storm debris – paper, plastic sheeting, foliage, dust, rain drops. The rain suddenly fell in thick waves on his windshield; trees swayed in the wind. Pellets of hail knocked against Grant's car. He heard Walt's voice on the radio, ordering all photographers to the storm zone if any were out and about. He reached for the microphone, put it to his mouth, then held it there for a moment before putting the mike back in its cradle.

He never saw a funnel, just the swirling, misty, jagged black clouds that carried the storm toward the north edge of the city. Now, he saw the aftermath. As he drove into a northeastern residential neighborhood as the storm continued raging northward, he saw the trees shorn of branches as though a mad chain saw artist had come deliberately and randomly hacking. Tree trunks leaned against porch roofs or across car tops and hoods.

Grant drove by a blue station wagon, saw movement at the window; he stopped. He peered out his side window and into the driver's side window of the station wagon. He saw a wad of curly gray hair, moving slightly. He turned on his emergency flashers and jumped out of his car. He ran to the station wagon, saw the old woman hovering inside. She had taken refuge from the storm in her station wagon. He knocked on the window; she peered up at him through misty, thick eyeglasses. He could see the rouge on her sunken cheeks, the gray bristle of her eyebrows, the flower pattern dress she wore, the outline of red lipstick around her mouth – she'd apparently just returned from shopping, or a garden club meeting, had seen the storm and decided to sit it out. Grant knocked again.

"Who are you?" she yelled through the glass.

Grant peered through the window at her.

"Go away!" she said.

Grant pulled on the door handle. She had locked it, apparently afraid that he might be a looter, a rapist, a madman come to do his damage after the storm. She shook visibly.

Grant smiled at her. He knocked again.

"I have a cell phone!" she shouted. "Leave me alone."

Grant backed away, turned and got back into his car. He was about to drive away when he looked across the seat and saw his camera bag. He unzipped it, grabbed a camera and ran back outside. He quickly set the camera for flash and focused, set his shutter speed and F stop; he aimed at the frightened woman who glared straight at the camera lens, her face frozen. He clicked the shutter, forwarded the film and shot again, filling the inside of her car with the lightening glare of his flash, then walked quickly back to his car and drove away, leaving the woman wondering what he'd been all about, who he was, peeking over the rim of the window until she discerned that he had gone away, then gathering her nerve and strength, pushing her car door open and pumping her legs as fast as they could carry her to the safety of her home.

As he drove through the storm ruins of the neighborhood, stopping to shoot photos, Grant felt as though he were traveling through a television program he'd watched, tapes he'd seen on the television news of storm damage in Mississippi or Texas, newsreels of the ravages of tornadoes with the voice-overs of basso news anchors reading text of copy describing wind-shorn trees, hail-mauled homes, storm-damaged automobiles, flooding streets, shattered windows, broken arms and legs, people killed in flipped automobiles. He drove through neighborhoods where men were already out with their chain saws, severing limbs from trees, hacking tree parts into logs, dragging branches into the street for city crews to haul away. He saw neighbors sitting on porches, surveying their damaged homes and cars as they drank hot coffee, smoked cigarettes – some of them laughed, thanking God, uttering the phrase over and over: It could have been worse.

Everywhere, the ground was muddy, lawns torn up, trees ripped apart – in front of one house, the wind had uprooted a 60-foot oak, tearing up the gutter and sidewalk with it, laying the tree parallel to the sidewalk leading to the front porch, its upper trunk and limbs resting on top of the roof as through to provide shelter from the rain for those wishing to enter the house. Ambulances wailed in the air, joining with the sound of chain saws roaring, neighbors bellowing and the patter of rainfall.

Grant took all of his pictures to the newspaper office – the shots he'd taken that morning at the turkey plant, where company officials, eager for positive publicity following the federal raid, had opened their doors to Grant, allowing him to shoot any subject, any worker on the premises, any operation – and the pictures he'd taken that afternoon of the storm damage. He and Tracy were the only photographers to respond to Walt's radio call; another shooter was on vacation, one was on assignment in another town, one was on night duty and home asleep with his telephone switched off.

At that afternoon's budget meeting, Fisher looked through the stack of storm photos for about 15 minutes before selecting two for the front page – one, shot by Grant, of a blooming yellow geranium standing intact next to the uprooted remains of an old elm tree, the other a photo by Tracy of medical personnel wrapping the broken arm of a man whose car had slammed into an abandoned warehouse as he tried to avoid a falling tree.

Grant kept for himself the photo of the woman he'd come across in the station wagon.

After selecting the front page stories and photos – the storm and its sidebars made up the bulk of the front page – Fisher looked at Walt as the photo chief stood up to leave the budget meeting.

"Let's get some more pictures for the next day's paper, we'll do a picture page of folks cleaning up the storm," he said. "Baker got some good shots. See what a little pep talk can do now and then?"

The editor gave Walt a quick, dark wink of his eye, then stood up and followed his photo chief out of the conference room. Walt saw Grant standing in the photo department and gave him a thumbs up.

Grant drove home in a light drizzle that covered the city in a hazy mist. He found Pauline in the kitchen cutting up a salad. Water was in a silver pot to boil.

"I thought I'd make some spaghetti," Pauline said.

Making spaghetti meant opening a jar of sauce, mixing in some pre-sliced mushrooms and pouring it over pasta, with a side of pre-cut tossed salad, sliced tomatoes, cucumbers, more mushrooms, doused in bottled light Italian dressing. Grant put on a Dave Brubeck album; he sat in the dark living room and listened to Paul Desmond play his alto saxophone all around Brubeck's piano chords. Jazz like this, where the musicians, even in the studio, rely on their feelings, their moods, command of technique, to improvise on a musical theme, was a perishing art form – like black and white newspaper photography, replaced by splashy color, bright reds and blues and yellows to make the front page look like a spring flower garden instead of a news report requiring thoughtful reading and analysis. Electronics, computers, had invaded and permeated jazz; pianists now played electronic keyboards with no pedals, no key action; photographers played on the computer with color, tone and shading levels to maximize the hues of a photograph – no more dodging or burning in the darkroom to create heightened and lowered black and white contrast to shape the mood of a photo without altering its image.

Grant was getting old, with no voice to

protest the changing times.

As Desmond bounced a solo through Grant's living room speakers, the photographer gazed at the window, saw the rain falling down the dark pane in tiny rivulets like the track of a tear from a big brown eye. Suddenly, he stood up. He went into the kitchen, to his film drawer, and took out spools of black and white film, which he took to his camera tote and stuffed into a side pocket.

"This spaghetti's ready," Pauline announced, dishing salad and forking noodles onto a plate. She poured a glass of water and motioned for Grant to take his place at the table. Grant obeyed. He sat down, sprinkled packaged parmesan cheese onto his sauce, swallowed vinegary salad greens and tomatoes, as he planned out his night's photo shoot.

"You going back out tonight?" Pauline said.

Grant nodded.

"Work? Or your own stuff?"

No response.

Pauline sighed. "Doesn't matter," she said. "That was some storm today. Elaine Strickland has a house in the neighborhood that was hit. Do you know if they officially declared it a tornado or not? The radio on the way home was saying most of the damage seemed to be straight-line winds."

Grant ate his spaghetti as Pauline talked. The sauce was tangy, sharp. He liked it. Prepared spaghetti sauce had evolved well from the canned noodles and meat sauce he'd eaten as a kid; the stuff in the jar now was almost good enough to forego making your own sauce – though some Sunday afternoons, Grant still enjoyed slicing up spaghetti sauce ingredients, sipping on a cold beer, listening to the jazz on his kitchen CD player, and sitting down to a homemade meal of pasta.

"The radio said the governor's sending some people over tomorrow to survey the damage and to maybe declare a disaster, which means we'd get some state money. Our house didn't get any damage, just a few flower pots blown over on the front porch." Pauline stirred her salad vegetables into the dressing, then did the same with the noodles and the sauce. She liked to mix her food, to blend it on the plate before it reached her stomach; she took a few bites of spaghetti, then some salad, then a bite of buttered bread, then a drink of water. Grant ate his salad first, then the spaghetti, mopped up the sauce with his bread, then washed it all down with his water. "I want to call Elaine later tonight to see how bad her damage was. I guess you got a bunch of pictures for the paper. The radio said there were only a couple of injuries. That's good. So I guess, even if it was a tornado, it wasn't a killer tornado. So we probably won't be a disaster in the governor's eyes, is my guess. Of course, it would be a disaster if this same storm hit the state capital."

Grant drank his water and stood up. He leaned over Pauline and gave her a kiss on the cheek, then grabbed his camera tote. He went to the closet by the back door and took out his work jacket – a fishing vest he'd bought long ago, covered with buttoned pockets and inside compartments for lures and hooks and other gear, only Grant used it for filters and lens covers and exposed film. He looked at his wife and waved goodbye.

"I'll be in bed when you come home, probably," she said. "I'll try and stay awake for you. Although it doesn't matter. I wake up when you come in anyway, no matter what time it is. I don't sleep well when you're not in the house."

Pauline didn't sleep well anytime.

Grant headed downtown, eyeing the night through the windshield as he drove. Because the newspaper publisher had relocated the plant in a suburban industrial park, with his own ten acres of greenery and bike and walking trails and picnic area, it had been some time since Grant had been downtown, in the center of the city. Years ago, newspapers were in the heart of the city, along with city hall, the county courthouse, the federal office buildings, the major banks and businesses all within walking distance. Now, everything is all spread out – good for the weekly mileage sheets, but hard on time and schedules.

Downtown was still dripping from the storm. Vacant offices were scattered among the brick, cement, glass and steel buildings. The bars were open, their neon signs twisted into red, orange, yellow, blue lettering proclaiming brands of beer. Grant parked his car in a two-hour zone, grabbed some rolls of film, his camera and flash, and he set out on foot to explore the city – a black-and-white exploration of the lights, the wetness everywhere, the streets still moist, the buildings washed clean and blown dry by the afternoon winds, then rinsed again in the soft rain that followed the main storm.

Everything was glistening – the glass, the chrome of the cars parked along the streets, the lights that shone on street corners. Grant went to the closest corner, where a black pole supported a white, round light that hung down; behind the streetlight, a tower of office buildings was all lit up; he focused his camera and shot the lights from beneath the streetlight, so that the streetlight stood above the building in the perspective of the photo like a moon, an artificial, electrically powered moon illuminating the city – with a wide, black expanse of sky behind it like a canvas of a painting.

It had been a long time since Grant had shot black and white merely for black and white, concentrating on focus, perspective, contrast, light and shadow.

He walked two blocks, found a couple of cops sitting in a cruiser, sipping from white styrofoam cups of coffee that steamed in the cool, damp night. He smiled at them; they smiled back as he focused his camera on the black-and-white patrol car, on the policemen, one black, one white, both of them wearing black-and-white uniforms, and on the steam that rose out of their cups of fresh coffee.

Except for the neon tubing in shop and tavern windows, the whole city was black and white at night.

Grant walked a couple more blocks. He stopped, turned around, saw the skyline poking into the air, which was misty in the lights of the city, thick and humid and hazy, other-worldly – it evoked in Grant an image of what nighttime London might have looked like in an old English murder mystery, the air chilly and wet, eerie. The buildings probed the sky, a hodge-podge of sharp, angular lines and corners, a geometric jumble, a mural of brick and cement and glass, the lights in the windows blurry and soft. Grant got down on his knees and aimed his camera at the cityscape, at the moment, at the urban counterpart of a mountainscape with square, black peaks instead of rugged, triangular purple ones; the scene was almost a black-and-white watercolor glowing with the brightness and glare of a city just showered and ready for sleep.

Across the street, the dark, tinted windows of a high rise stood on top of the city's cement base like a steel and glass tower of granite. Grant crossed the still, deserted pavement. He stopped a couple of feet from the glass, stared at the tiny droplets of water that clung to the juncture of glass and cement. He replaced his lens with a zoom and focused on the water beads – they contained lights, the colored neon of the windows up and down the street, the steady white of the streetlights, the wide, expansive mist of the sky, all of it holding the lights and reflections of the entire city and its apartments and homes and cars and music and drinking and dancing and sobbing, of the stars and the galaxies draped by the noisy, bustling light of the city merging with the refracted and reflected illumination of the universe and of all time. For a moment, all was silent. The beads of water on the window contained universal eternity viewed through the telescopic microscope of Grant's camera – all being and non-being was in a drop of water at the moment that Grant photographed, that his shutter clicked open and shut like a portal to timelessness and forever – a drop of water clinging to a sheet of glass like billions of drops grasping tree leaves, strands of hair, shards of rock, clumps of earth, rusty piles of scrap, emerging stalks of corn, marble columns of architecture all over the planet – everything contained in a single drop of water in that moment.

"What the hell you doing with that camera?"

The voice, deep, sudden, boomed in the still night behind Grant. He whirled around, saw the uniform of a man, apparently a security guard, then the uniform cap, the black belt, the holster with its bright gun with a black handle, the goggles, the polished black shoes.

"I asked you a question, mister."

Grant looked back at the man, who stepped forward.

"What business you got here, takin' pictures of the inside of this office? What you got there, some kind of infrared lens or something, can see through tinted glass?"

The man stood a few feet from Grant, his face thick, rigid, pale.

"We can do this easy," the man said. "You can tell me what the hell you're up to. Or we can do it hard."

Grant watched the man; the man watched Grant. The only sound was a clicking of glass against glass somewhere, likely a couple of bar mates toasting each other.

The man stepped toward Grant and shoved him lightly. Grant stepped back. The man shoved him again, then again, down the sidewalk, out of the glow of the streetlight, toward an alley. The recess of the alley was dark, a portal of blackness. The man pushed Grant toward the alley, then into it.

He put his face into Grant's so that Grant could feel his hot breath.

"One more time, what the hell you doing

here with that camera?"

Grant reached behind him for his wallet, his press card.

"Oh no you don't, you Arab son of a bitch!"

The photographer felt a thud on his head, then saw the guard's raised arm, the stick in his hand, saw it come down, felt himself going down beneath it. Then he saw a windshield coming at him, a girl behind the glass, screaming toward him, heard tires skidding, the shattering of the glass, the thump of tires leaving pavement, the crash of metal, a moan, a long, painful, sobbing, plaintive moan. Then he heard Pauline's voice. He saw whiteness, a light, bright, going on and off like a strobe piercing the blackness, then realized he was blinking, peering through wetness, through teary eyes at whiteness, at a group of people around him. He saw Walt, men in blue pants and shirts, Pauline, her eyes looking into his face. Grant realized he was in an emergency room. He grabbed his head, which was white, like the light, with pain. A woman in white, her hair gray and silver, bent over him, looking into his eyes, into his face.

"What kind of assignment was he on?" It was Pauline's voice.

"I don't know," came Walt's reply in his

slow, stammering mumble. "Derek told me to have them shoot some storm cleanup pictures, you know, aftermath kind of stuff. That's what I told him to look for."

"Walt, he was found in an alley downtown, bleeding from the head."

"I'm sorry, Pauline, that's all I know."

Grant stared at Pauline's face. He realized he was on his back, on a table of some kind, with white curtains on either side of him.

Pauline's face was in his, looking down at him; he could see the glow of a light bulb above her, backlighting her face so that it had an outline, like a pencil drawing on white paper.

"They say you got a knock on the head," Pauline told him. "That's all. Somebody hit you on the head, Grant. The man who found you, he was coming out of a bar. He found your wallet next to you. All your money was in it. Your camera had been smashed. But nothing else, Grant. Grant, what were you doing downtown?"

Grant shook his head; he felt like his brain was rattling inside. He stared at Pauline, watching her face as he closed his eyes and went to sleep.

"They want him to spend the night," Pauline said to Walt. "I'm going to stay here for awhile.

You go on home."

"He'll be alright, Pauline," Walt said.

"Walt, I don't want him going out on assignment at night anymore."

"Not even ball games?"

Pauline sighed. "Walt, I'm worried about him. Look at what happened tonight. We have no way of knowing how this happened. Why. Where. Somebody could have killed him."

"Somebody could kill any newspaper photographer, Pauline. There are people out there who just plain don't like us."

Pauline nodded her head. "I know."

"And he knows it, Pauline. Listen, I'll be careful what assignments I send him on. But you know as well as I do, he wouldn't want special treatment just cuz he can't talk. He's a newspaper photographer, Pauline, plain and simple. But I'll be more careful."

"Thanks, Walt."

Pauline sat down in a chair next to her husband's emergency room bed and watched him sleep, his head wrapped in white gauze. She tried to imagine what had happened to him – thugs looking for a handout – no, his wallet wasn't touched. Just some crazy guy out there who apparently didn't like photographers and their cameras was the best she could guess.

IX

As happens sometimes, a moment settled and hovered and remained for much more than a moment. And sound stopped and movement stopped for much, much more than a moment.

– John Steinbeck, Of Mice and Men

Grant opened his eyes to moonlight shining into his bedroom through the window in the wall opposite the bed. Someone was sitting in the easy chair in the corner, next to the desk. He recognized the piano playing of Oscar Peterson filling the room, like faraway music playing on the speaker of an elevator – a smooth, dark ride up the shaft of a modern, clean building. The piano notes plunked softly, like musical stars in the dark. The moonlight shone on the hair of his wife, the person in the easy chair.

"I brought your CD player up from the kitchen," Pauline said. She reached over and flicked on the floor lamp next to her. She sat in the chair in her sleeping shirt, her black hair shiny in the lamplight. "You've been asleep most of the day. The doctor said you got a mild concussion and that you would be sleeping a lot for a couple of days."

Grant sat up, fluffed his pillow behind him, then leaned back again, folding the top of the pillow into his neck for support. This was his nighttime television-watching position, when he lay straight back and watched the small portable color set on the top of the dresser. Only now he was watching Pauline instead, in the corner of the room opposite the television. A steady ache sat on the top of his head like painful noise.

"I've been sitting here watching and listening to you sleep," Pauline said. "You still snore, Grant. You still make noise out of your mouth. And I've been trying to figure out what happened to you. You went out to take pictures, then I'm called to the hospital where you've been mugged or beaten up or something. And nobody knows what happened except that your camera was smashed. So I have to use my wits and my imagination to figure it out. And you know me, Grant. I always imagine the worst. I imagined that you were in the apartment of some woman, her husband or boyfriend came home unexpectedly and found you there, and he beat you up and dragged you out to the street. But then I lose that image, because you told me once that you would never screw around again. Remember that? Remember when you took me out to dinner that night, and then for dessert, over wine, confessed that you had been with another woman? Then we had a good cry together, remember? And you promised that you'd never do it again. I asked you why you had told me; why, since you had decided not to do it again, you bothered to tell me about it. Guilt, you said. The guilt was driving you crazy. So you told me; you let me have my own guilt. You let me believe that I had driven you to another woman, that I had done something wrong, that I was inadequate – that something was wrong with me. But then, you know that's how I am. Guilty. That was seven years ago, Grant, and I do believe you've kept your promise. But how do I know?"

Pauline blinked. Grant saw the dampness in her eyes, her hand go to her face to wipe at the corner of each eye.

"So then I imagine that you were minding your own business, taking pictures, and some men came along demanding money, and when you were unable to respond to them, they beat you up. Only, Grant, there was no money missing from your wallet. At least, there was some money still in it; I assume muggers would have taken it all. Whoever did this to you only broke your camera, so they weren't after your money. Then I think maybe you're working on an assignment for the paper that has somebody pissed off – but Walt said no, just a news feature on some migrant workers and their children. And that one's over and done. So apparently, whatever happened last night, only you know why and how it happened. Maybe you'll tell me someday, maybe not."

Pauline got up from the chair and came to the bed. She sat down next to Grant, reached out and touched his leg. She rubbed her hand up and down it gently.

"You know I've forgiven you for what happened before," she said. "I'm only telling you the thoughts that have entered my mind, the wild things I've imagined trying to figure out what happened. You remember, Grant, once I told you the only thing I would never forgive would be if you went to another woman. Obviously, I didn't know what I was talking about. I still love you – more than before, Grant. You could probably do it again and you'd still find me here at home waiting for you." She smiled at her husband. "You're stuck with me, Grant."

Pauline leaned over and kissed Grant on the forehead, then went back to the chair. Oscar

THE SILENT TREATMENT

Peterson's piano notes lingered in the room, the sweetest piano playing Grant had heard in a long time. He lay on his back; his eyes closed; he remembered Nadine, her brown hair parted in the middle and falling in waves over her shoulders, her thin body. She worked in the lab at the newspaper; she and her husband had just filed for divorce. She and Grant were in the photo lab alone one night; she started talking about her husband, about how they had married too soon, both to escape unhappy lives at home with their parents, about how she came to understand within months that marriage does not bring happiness or even escape, that it can be just a different kind of miserable trap. Then she and Grant went out for beers – she said she liked the way he quietly listened to her, how he seemed to understand what she was saying about her marriage, about her husband, about how she missed certain parts of him but couldn't stand certain others – little things like food getting caught in his beard, bigger things like lack of fore and afterplay in their sex lives, even bigger things like dismissing her opinions as stupidity, her work as uninteresting, like leaving her at home on Friday nights while he went bar-hopping with his work buddies, like never accompanying her to visit her family across town, or being away when her parents came to her house. She liked Grant's photographs, liked to listen to him talk about some day showing his work in a gallery. Through it all, Grant bought her beers, told her his plans, and he listened to her, until one night she invited him to follow her home, to listen to a jazz record she'd found in a bargain bin at a record store; listening to the record turned into dancing to it and then making love to it – and Grant was attentive to her afterward, and she looked at him as they lay in her bed, and she told him he should do what he wanted to with his life because we only have this one go at it, told him if he ever found himself in a failed marriage that she would be there. And then her husband reentered her life; they decided it was worth one more try. Nadine told Grant over their last beers together that she needed to put their romance on hold, as though it were a housing plan or a proposed business merger, instead of his life.

Nadine was a long time ago, like a childhood dream that never comes back when you've grown up. Nadine and her husband stayed back together, she got a new job, and Grant lived for months with the guilt of her, keeping it inside of him, until he finally confessed, hoping that letting the guilt out would get rid of it – promising himself, after Pauline's tears, that next time he would just keep quiet and learn to live with the guilt. And then promising himself there would be no next time.

Grant lay in his bedroom, with Pauline sitting quietly in the corner, and he replayed the memory of sitting in a suburban bar with Nadine. Country music twanged on a juke box that emitted blue light in a corner of the bar by the front door. Men and women in blue jeans, boots, tennis shoes, lined the bar, sitting behind glasses of beer, shots of whiskey. Nadine ran her index finger around the rim of her glass, its yellow liquid reflecting the lights of the bar signs. Grant sipped his beer and studied Nadine's face, its sloping jaw, its clear complexion and high cheek bones, the eyes that were brown and white ovals that blinked at him as Nadine talked softly, words he could not comprehend; he felt a pang in his chest as he watched her lips move – she spoke slowly, deliberately, and he couldn't understand a word she was saying because the pool balls were crashing in the back of the room, men were guffawing, a steel guitar moaned through the place.

He watched the pool balls gathered like shining marbles strewn about a neatly clipped lawn, the white cue ball was like a big balloon, dusty ivory floating across the wide, long, green felt of the pool table; the black eight ball hit the bank and then floated into the air, upward, toward the ceiling, beyond the ceiling and into the sky; and then Grant was the eight ball, soaring toward clouds, then above them so that he was a black speck in a vast blue sky with a searing orange sun in the distance; and then he was falling, flapping his arms like a bird with wounded wings; Air Force jets were closing in on him, screaming around him; a dove came next to him and he remembered the face of the dove, its black eyes surrounded by clean white feathers, peering at him, its beak sharp, brittle; the dove flew at him as the din of the jets grew louder until a metal wing clipped the dove, severing its head. Blood spewed from its neck as the dove's detached head fixed its gaze on Grant, the bird, the head and Grant falling toward the ground as Grant strained against the looming crash into the earth, he pulled and pulled backward and then opened his eyes, blinking them slowly, his heart pulsing as the roar of the jets faded, the bird plummeted to the ground and he was in his bedroom, his and Pauline's bedroom.

"Have a nice sleep?" Pauline said. She sat

in the same chair as before, the lamp shining on her from the side. Her shadow on the wall next to the desk was large, a black continent surrounded by a sea of dim yellow light. An open book lay on her lap.

"David called today," she said. "He won't be coming home this summer. One of his friends at college has hooked him up with a construction job in his home town. But he said to tell you hello and he'll be able to make it for July Fourth."

Grant watched Pauline's shadow, the large head move, as she talked. The room was quiet otherwise. Beyond the window, a semi roared on the state route that passed through the city a couple of blocks away. Children yelped in a yard across the street; a dog barked along with them.

Grant had been paying more attention to sounds, to the input function of his brain, since he'd stopped speaking.

Pauline was thumbing through a photo album on her lap. She stood up and carried it to the bed. She flicked on the overhead light, filling the room with brightness, then sat down on the bed next to Grant, who was still propped partway up on his pillow.

"I came across this in the basement," she said, opening the album. On the first page were pictures of David as a baby. In one of the pictures, hands, Pauline's hands, were bathing a naked infant David in the kitchen sink.

"Remember that apartment? It was up on the third floor of that old mansion, and the doctor's office was on the second floor. You talked the landlord into letting you set up a darkroom in the basement. You used to strap David onto your back in that little baby carrier we had, and then we'd go into the city, or the country, and you'd take pictures. We'd stop and eat our lunch at a park, I packed us sandwiches or we bought a bucket of Kentucky Fried. You loved David so much when he was a baby."

Grant watched as Pauline flipped through the pages of the photo album, watched his son slowly grow up – pictures of birthday parties, a shiny red tricycle, then a new black bicycle, David in a little-league baseball uniform.

"Remember that year you helped coach?" Pauline stopped at the baseball picture. "You were determined to do everything you could to make sure every kid got playing time. That one Saturday, Lou Henry the head coach had to be out of town, he asked you to take over the team. You worked on that lineup for two hours, working it out so that every kid on the team was in the game for at least half the time." Pauline chuckled. "Afterward, after we lost, the father of one of the regular players came screaming at you for taking his kid out of the game in the fourth inning. He said you were destroying his son's baseball career. Remember that? His son's baseball career – in what, the sixth grade was it? That was the only game the team lost that year. The next time Lou couldn't be there, he asked the other guy, you remember, that fat kid's dad, to coach the team. And he left a lineup behind and told him to follow it."

Pauline moved to the next page, and the next. A photo of David, his hair black like his mother's, cut short, at the piano the day of a recital. He wore a little blue sport coat, a white shirt and a brown tie to go with his tan slacks.

"You know," Pauline said, "they say a picture never lies. But neither does it tell all the truth. Look how happy David looks in this picture. I remember that day. David played that song he liked, I don't remember the name of it, kind of classical. And then he missed a couple of notes. And then another. He panicked then, remember? He panicked, started over, missed the same two notes again, then finally worked his way through the song. Remember? You guys fought afterward, over practice time. You told him that if he'd practiced the song the way he was supposed to, he wouldn't have missed those two notes. Remember? You increased his practice time from a half hour to an hour a day – and you two fought over that piano for the next three years, until you finally let him quit the piano. But it wasn't just the piano. You fought over everything after that – he watched too much television, he didn't study hard enough. And he gave it right back to you, too. He'd catch you watching television, and he thought that was hypocritical because you didn't like him watching it."

Pauline slowly shook her head, then smiled. "I was the family referee in those days. Sometimes I felt like I was stopping two kids from fighting. I don't know what it was with you two, both of you feeling like it was the other one's fault, like the other one didn't love you, when really you both did love each other. You know that now. At least I hope you know that now."

Pauline turned more pages, and David grew into a teenager and then a young man. He posed in his prom tuxedo, in his graduation gown, standing by his first car – photographs shot by Grant, chronicling the growing-up of his son as any father takes photos, or video camera documentaries, of his children as they move through the important events of their lives, the photographs serving as touchstones, only as reminders, of times and scenes and events that were so much more – that were joyous occasions, milestones, or only posed smiles punctuating tumultuous, bickering years of an unhappy youth.

Pauline closed the book as Grant's soft snoring filled the room. She went back to her chair and sat, watching her husband sleep off his concussion, wondering again how he'd gotten bopped on the head and why.

Grant walked the halls of his high school. The green tile floor looked freshly waxed; it shone as though a spring rain had just fallen inside the building and frozen over. He peered into a classroom, saw his father lecturing a roomful of students. His father looked out the open doorway at Grant, smiled and then talked to him, mouthing words that Grant could not hear, speaking silently. Grant lifted his camera, aimed and shot his father, who looked at Grant. His father's face was suddenly wrinkled, his hair gray, his jowls hanging loosely from his cheeks, as Grant had seen his father on his death bed. Then Grant was in the cafeteria, he was at a lectern, speaking to students, teachers. He held up a photo, told them the photo is life, a life captured on paper, on film, displayed for the world. Lived correctly, it could be a good life, a good photograph; he told them that even the best photographs, though, can have contrast, can have light and darkness – and that is what makes a good photograph; the shadows, the darkness, enhances the light, makes it brighter, bolder. Just like the contrasts are what make life so sweet. The room applauded Grant.

Then Grant was going home from school, lugging his books, walking through his childhood neighborhood, seeing the details of the houses of his youth – Mrs. Rodney's golden marigolds behind the white picket fence, Mr. Gantner sitting on his porch in a rocking chair smoking his pipe, the black Labrador behind the chain link fence barking at every footstep – and he heard his father's voice, all around him, soft and firm. His father had never yelled at him; he commanded attention by speaking in a low tone, distinctly and clearly, slowly, so that you stopped and listened to each word.

But it was a gentle voice.

"Just swing and hit the ball, partner." His father tossed a tennis ball at him; Grant swung and smacked it, giggling as his father ran across the street, retrieved the ball, then walked back to the yard that was green and fresh and surrounded by trees and by the irises and roses and snap dragons and petunias his father had planted. "That was good, partner, real good. Now keep your eye on the ball like that every time."

Then Grant was a little boy in his father's office. His father sat in a swivel chair in his work suit, a brown jacket and slacks, black tie, white shirt, behind the desk where he took money from people wanting to protect themselves against catastrophe, accidents, bad luck.

"Beating God's odds," his father said of his work in the insurance business as he sat on the front porch on a summer night, sipping a cold beer and sucking on a Camel.

"Beating God's odds." The voice filled Grant's head like a scratchy 78-rpm phonograph record as he opened his eyes in his bedroom.

He lay on his pillow staring upward in the dark room, remembering his father's voice.

"Newspaper photography is a noble enough profession I suppose. But you won't make any money." His father took a puff of his cigarette, then spit a piece of tobacco from his mouth – the single dominant image Grant carried of his father. "I've got a client in the news business. I know. Not only does he make a lousy salary, but he's a drunk. Why would you choose a profession like that? Taking pictures of other people living their lives, of crooked politicians and greedy athletes and stuck-up celebrities. Think, kid, think."

Grant felt Pauline next to him, the rhythm of her breathing. Outside the open window, a car pulled up to the stop sign. A bluesy harmonica spilled out its window as the driver revved the engine, squealed the tires and drove into the next block, trailing the harmonica music that filled the air with its plaintive, lonely screech.

Pauline lay her hand across his stomach.

"I heard your eyes open," she said.

Grant glanced at her, then returned his gaze to the ceiling, to the outline of the glass lampshade that covered the unlit bulb.

"Y'know, Grant, this silence of yours really doesn't change our lives that much. I've been thinking about it. The last few years, we haven't really talked that much to each other, y'know? I've talked to you. And talked and talked. But you haven't done much talking back to me. When I think about it, you mainly just listen to me. It's been a long time since we've sat down and really talked to each other, listened to each other. Y'know?"

Grant felt Pauline's fingers tighten on his

stomach. She sat up, looked down into his face.

"Why didn't you just tell me to shut up sometimes?"

She lay back into her pillow, and they both watched the dark ceiling, the shadows that moved across it as a car approached from the far end of the street and then turned off at the corner.

"But then, I guess in your own way, you did. I could tell when you were just ignoring me, hoping I'd just talk myself out. I guess it happens to all marriages. The two just settle into their routines, go off into their own thoughts, they talk to each other less, and what they do say isn't much worth saying. That's about where we were, Grant. So I guess maybe there's something to learn from this. Maybe I can learn to keep my thoughts to myself – like you're doing. Say something when it's important. Like I love you, and we'll get through this just like we've gotten through everything else."

Grant felt Pauline's head turn toward him, then her body. She put her arm around Grant and pulled him to her so that they were parallel on the bed, curled into each other, and they both fell asleep that way in the quiet early morning bedroom.

X

If there were a little more silence, if we all kept quiet... maybe we could understand something.

– Federico Fellini

Piano chords and violin strings filled the newspaper lobby. The afternoon sun poured in through the windows, glinting off the wine glasses of the newspaper guests as they strolled among the photographs displayed on the easels spread about the room and on the white, square columns of the immense, red-tiled lobby. Derek Fisher stood in the middle of it all, glass of white wine in hand, wearing a black, collarless shirt with pearl buttons all the way up to the neck. Over the shirt he wore a white sport coat, and beneath it a pair of white slacks – he was a living, black-and-white personification of the largely black-and-white photography on display. He smiled down upon the wispy, blonde woman who faced him. She wore a glass of red wine in her right hand, a bright ruby ring on the third finger of her left hand, and a black dress that was slit

THE SILENT TREATMENT

up the side.

"You'd never know how much he hated the Metro, the way he's cozying up to its arts writer," said Walt, who stood with Grant near the door that entered the newsroom. They each held a can of light beer. Walt wore a pair of tan slacks, brown loafers and a blue shirt held together at the top by the knot of a necktie. Grant was in his gray pinstripe suit, his only suit, bought five years ago when he attended a ceremony in the state capitol to accept a first-place state Associated Press award for feature photography. His red necktie matched the ruby of the blonde woman talking to Derek Fisher. A bandage above and in front of Grant's right ear was the only visible reminder of his recent bout with a downtown security guard.

Scattered about the room were various members of the city's residents who had accepted the newspaper's invitation, offered to the public at large in a six column by 10 inch ad announcing the kickoff installment of the newspaper's six-part series on immigrant workers that Sunday, along with the opening that afternoon of the newspaper's latest exhibit in its lobby – free and open to the public, along with a cash bar and some finger food – cheese, grapes, dips – courtesy of the Bulletin. The exhibit offered the unpublished photographs that Grant Baker had taken to accompany the immigrant series. Copies of that day's newspaper were stacked next to the front door, free for the taking – and there on the front page was Grant's depiction of immigrant village life, along with part one of Ralston's series, headlined: "Aliens among us." Below the bold, 72-point headline was the subhead: "The land of plenty comes up short in the region's migrant worker community." A black framed box explained that the six-part series was an examination of the plight of the children of the area's legal immigrant workers from south of the U.S. border – laborers who toil for low wages, live in substandard housing and require large tax expenditures for their special educational needs and social services.

Ralston circulated among the guests – county commissioners, state legislators, a representative from a U.S. senator's office, members of the clergy, a smattering of minorities, a few artsy types.

"Look at her," Walt said, watching the blonde in the black dress. "Her rag slings arrows at us every chance it gets, and she shows up and schmoozes with the editor. He's loving it."

Fisher, a black-and-white stack of powerful triangles standing in the center of his editorial palace, smiled and joked with Lindsay Cameron, the Metro's art critic; he took her empty wine glass, walked authoritatively to the bar and ordered another, then returned to her and handed the sparkling glass to her with a slight bow.

"I'd love to hear the bullshit coming out of that little conversation," Walt said. "She's been wanting to get on with this newspaper for years, and from the looks of things she's ready to do whatever necessary to spice up her resume. You want another beer?" Without waiting for a response, Walt took Grant's empty bottle and headed to the bar for a couple of refills.

He returned just as Derek Fisher and Lindsay Cameron were heading Grant's way.

"I want you to meet the man who took these photographs," the editor said, touching the art critic's elbow with his fingers and gently guiding her along. She moved smoothly in her black dress, as though she were sliding on a set of invisible wheels. Grant watched the blonde hair, cut in a straight mop just even with the bottom of her ears, her thick lips painted red, the lids of her eyes wearing a light green tint. Baby crows feet had just begun to sprout at the corners of her eyes.

"This is wonderful work," Lindsay said to

Grant, holding out her hand to be shaken. "I love black-and-white photography, when used discriminately, as you've done."

She smiled at Grant. She was short, the top of her head level with Grant's eyes, and thin. She could have hidden easily behind the muscular Derek Fisher, had the editor ordered the room into an impromptu game of hide and seek.

"Grant Baker, Lindsay Cameron," the editor said, unhanding Lindsay and depositing her in front of Grant and Walt. "Grant has taken some of our more important photographs over the years," the editor said, stepping back from the quartet. "But I'm sure you knew that already, as an informed and critical reader of our – what does your editorial page call it? Ah, yes, our yellow-tinted rag."

Lindsay smiled. "Grant, I've long been a fan of your work – and of your newspaper. I don't write the Metro's editorials and don't often agree with them. I just write about art."

"I'll leave you visual experts alone," Derek Fisher said.

"Don't forget lunch sometime," the art critic said.

"Just phone my secretary," the editor said as he turned to leave. "She knows my schedule."

Grant watched as his boss walked toward a group of elected officials gathered at one of the photographs – a picture of the turkey plant at dusk, the sun rising behind it.

"Asshole," Lindsay said. "He'll get lunch with me the day the Bulletin supports a Democrat for president. Not in my lifetime."

Lindsay wove her arm around Grant's and guided him toward one of the photographs. "Please tell me about your work."

"Uh," Walt said.

"Yes?" Lindsay smiled at him.

"Nothing," Walt said. "I'll talk to you later Grant."

Lindsay tugged Grant gently toward an easel. They stopped about five feet away and studied the image of a teenage Hispanic woman, dressed in a red blouse with its sleeves rolled up to the elbows, a cigarette dangling from her heavily lipsticked mouth.

"One of the rare color photos in the set," Lindsay said, gazing at the picture.

Grant studied Lindsay's face. It was thin, with strong cheekbones beneath eyes that were a couple of shades bluer than the sky beyond the windows. Her eyelashes were thick, her eyebrows thin and blonde. She wore no jewelry besides her red ring and no makeup beyond her lips and eyelids.

"But your use of color in this one is bold," she said. "The red lips and red shirt really stand out next to the drab world around her. She stands out. You're really good at bringing out shadows and depth. Did you use a filter with this?"

Grant looked at the photograph without answering.

"What, you the strong silent type?" Lindsay said. "Or you don't want to reveal trade secrets, or what?"

"He doesn't talk."

Grant and Lindsay turned around to see Ralston standing behind them.

"Hello Lindsay. Haven't seen you since, oh, two nights ago at the Club Cafe?" The reporter smiled, exhibiting a row of clean, white teeth.

"Hello Ralsty," Lindsay said. "What do you mean he doesn't talk?"

"Just what I said," Ralston said. "He just lost his voice one day."

"Oh?" The art critic eyed Grant up and down.

"The rest of him works fine," Ralston said. He laughed.

"How do you know?" Lindsay said.

"Trust me."

"I need a cigarette," Lindsay said.

"I'll walk you outside," Ralston said. "I could use some air."

Grant watched the two of them walk away. He glanced around the room, saw small groups of people gathered at each of his photos – pictures of men in cowboy and baseball hats hosing down turkey pens, a worker with blood-spattered hands and work clothes grinning into the camera, a grandmother walking down the village street hand-in-hand with a young girl in a white dress, a woman in a bloody apron chopping a turkey into pieces, a dog nosing among the turkey plant's trash bins, a photo of a female teacher leaning over a young boy as he tries to decipher the words in a book. They were photographs that told a story of poverty, of children raised caringly despite financial hardship, of families surviving on kinship and love, of pride of work, of slaughter, of simple pleasures.

Grant found Walt leaning against a wall a few feet from the bar. The photo chief had a fresh beer waiting for Grant. The two of them sipped their drinks and watched the crowd mingle, listened to the chatter of the room, the violins purring from the speakers installed in the room's walls, the pained exclamations of the politicians as they discussed the woes portrayed in the photographs on display and accompanying Ralston's stories. They watched Derek Fisher pump hands, shake his head sympathetically and understandingly as various folks stopped by to express their dismay over the plight of the immigrants – and over the taxpayers who supported them.

"What a fuckin' charade," Walt said. "I mean, your photos are good, Grant, don't get me wrong. And Ralston, as usual, did first-rate work even if he does say so himself. But this whole goddam show – I mean look at 'em. Here they are all dressed up, drinking wine, heading out to their expensive houses, probably going out to dinner at a nice restaurant. They don't give a shit about what's going on in that village. They don't care if those people have good medical care, if their kids are getting educated. And right there, our leader is heading up the whole goddam farce. He'll ride this thing all the way to the state awards banquet next year, he'll take home his goddam bonus for bringing more awards to the Bulletin, he'll write his editorials bemoaning the poverty and sickness and exploitation of the workers at the turkey plant – and all the time, Grant, he and the family that owns this newspaper are doing the same thing to us. Man, don't get me started."

Grant said nothing to get Walt started, just listened and watched. Finally, as the guests began to disperse – about the time the bar was closing down – Ralston emerged from a pack of people and headed toward Walt and Grant.

"This is good shit, man," Ralston said to Grant. "I mean it. We made a damn good team on this."

"Good job," Walt said. "Really."

"Thanks. Listen, buddy, I'm headin' downtown to the Club Cafe. I'll get you home if you want to ride along."

Grant looked at Walt, who had brought him.

"Hey, I'm goin' home is all," Walt said. "You guys should celebrate. This is your show."

"C'mon." Ralston took Grant by the arm and led him to the exit. Fisher had long ago departed; a few lingerers stood by the bar, persuading the barkeeper to part with one last glass of wine – red will do if the white's gone – or bottle of beer – sure, I'll take a regular if you're out of light.

Ralston grabbed the freeway south to downtown. The sun was low in the western sky, in which a few puffy, cumulous clouds hung like shredded balls of cotton. The buildings of the city stood in the distant haze. Stevie Ray Vaughan played the blues on Ralston's radio.

"Hot damn, this is our town tonight," Ralston said. He produced a can of beer from his blazer pocket and took a drink. "I hate the newspaper business for the most part, but then days like this come along. Did you hear the radio this morning? The local PBS affiliate picked up my story – they even credited the Bulletin – and they got a quote from the governor's office saying he's going to open an investigation into the whole legal immigrant work issue. The feds'll probably get involved too. This is their territory, y'know."

Grant watched the countryside roll by, the tract housing developments that interrupted the flow of grass, bushes, trees and the occasional clumps of woods.

"Fisher pulled me aside and said he plans to enter this series into next year's Pulitzer competition. Hot damn, pal. The Pulitzer. Just to be nominated is a big deal."

Grant listened to the reporter talk as they came to the downtown exits. Ralston turned off and drove through a neighborhood of warehouses and abandoned apartment buildings, then turned again and followed the road into the city. Downtown was pretty much boarded up for the weekend, but the corner bar that was the Club Cafe was aglow with neon, its doors open, music seeping out onto the street, which was filled with parked cars.

Ralston found a spot about a block away. He tipped the last of the beer into his mouth, crushed the empty and tossed it onto the back floor. He undid his black necktie and hung it over the rear view mirror. Grant loosened his and unbuttoned his dress shirt at the neck.

The Club Cafe was jammed with people. Ralston spotted Tracy at a booth near the rear rest rooms, held up two fingers and motioned to Tracy to save a couple of spots. The photographer grinned and nodded and pointed to the bar, signaling Ralston that she was ready for a fresh beer.

"You go join Tracy," Ralston said. "I'll get us some beers."

Grant elbowed through a crowd of men and women standing between the bar and a row of tables. He slid into the booth opposite Tracy.

"Hey," Tracy said. "Good stuff. Damn good stuff."

Grant took a glance around the bar. The Club Cafe used to be a skid row shot-and-beer bar, gone derelict from the days it had been a warehouse neighborhood after-work beer joint that served lunches to the local workers. A couple of hippies bought the place in the early 1970s – the story was they did it with proceeds from a few good drug deals – just before city officials decided the old warehouse and skid row neighborhood would make a prime redevelopment project with federal money. Contractors turned the warehouses into loft apartments, entrepreneurs with Small Business Administration loans bought and leased the street-level storefronts, installing restaurants and various shops – and the Club Cafe quickly became the nightspot for the reborn neighborhood's artists, writers and professionals. The owners had restored and refinished much of the original interior, from the tinplate ceiling with its big wooden fans that stirred the mixture of tobacco and marijuana smoke in the place, to the ceramic tile floor with its intricate six-sided red and brown and pink and white mosaics. The booths next to the walls were solid wood; the jukebox was filled with the musical touchstones of the '60s and '70s. The owners had long ago hired managers to run the place and had semi-retired to their respective homes – a cabin in the hills and a downtown loft – to count their money, though they occasionally stopped in for a drink and to talk over old times with the long-time regulars.

Ralston arrived, carrying a tray of six beers. "I figure we might as well save ourselves a trip for refills," he said.

Tracy reached for her purse.

"Uh uh," Ralston said. "These are mine. You get the next round."

"I was just telling Grant here that I liked what I saw in today's paper," Tracy said. "Good writing. Good pictures. Makes me wish I'd been a bit more territorial when Walt first took this project away from me." Tracy glanced at Grant, who was studying the bar.

Joni Mitchell sang a jazzy tune on the speakers, one in each corner of the main bar, all focused on the center of the room. Waiters in ponytails and earrings and waitresses in crew cuts and blue jeans scurried about the place, carrying trays of beer and appetizers.

A man wearing a pair of tan corduroys and a matching jacket over a white T-shirt came and stood next to the table.

"Hell of a piece, Ralston," he said.

Ralston grinned and nodded. "Thanks. You know Tracy. Roger, this is Grant Baker. He did the photos for the story. Grant, this is Roger Bennings. Local lawyer."

The attorney stuck his hand out. Grant shook it, eyed the lawyer's freckled face, red ponytail and gold earring, then noticed a familiar blonde head behind Bennings. Lindsay Cameron was standing in a crowd near the end of the bar.

"Listen, I gotta run. Look forward to the rest of the series," Bennings said. "Oh say, Ralston, you got a minute?"

"Sure." The reporter stood up. He and Bennings walked slowly to the front of the bar, then outside.

"Local lawyer," Tracy said. "Huh. More accurately: Local shyster. Guy's got his hand in every development and business deal in town. Hasn't seen the inside of a courtroom since his days working for the county attorney's office when he prosecuted the same folks who sold him his weekend dope."

Grant watched Lindsay. She stood on the fringe of the circle, holding her glass of wine with one hand, running the index finger of her left hand around and around the rim of the wine glass.

The room was loud with conversation and laughter. A television set on a ledge above the bar beamed a rock band gyrating on a deserted city street, the camera moving in for a close-up of each player's head – zoom-ins of nose rings, gelled layers of black hair, a gleaming bald head with the tattoo of a snake around its perimeter, a broomstick-thin drummer with no shirt and a bald chest beating on his tom-toms as the juke box played a crooning Jackson Browne running on empty. Across from Grant, Tracy sat with her beer, the tiny golden bubbles rising in her glass. Her thick, light brown hair was pulled into a ponytail that hung just below the shoulders of her white button-down shirt.

"How'd you talk Walt into giving you that immigrant gig anyway?" Tracy said, taking a gulp of her beer. "Aw shit, I'm sorry. I didn't mean that."

Grant ignored the comment and took his own swig, a long shot of beer. The Club Cafe did it right; the beer was cold and good. It had been a long time since Grant had gone to a bar with his fellow workers and just sat and drunk beer. He drained his glass and opened the second bottle, pouring it in slowly, watching the foam gather at the top and then sipping it off like a kid sucking whipped cream from the crest of a banana split.

Tracy drank down beer as the noise of the place swirled around her and Grant. She drained her bottle, then looked across the table at her fellow photographer. "Goddam loud in here," she said. "Could drive a person deaf."

Tracy grinned. "Not a bad idea. I go deaf, then maybe Walt'll throw a plum assignment my way. Excuse me. I see someone I need to talk to." The younger photographer carried her beer away from the booth, leaving it to Grant. A waiter walked by; Grant held up his bottle of beer. The waiter nodded and scurried to the bar to fill his orders.

"Join you?"

Grant recognized the voice, what little he'd heard of it that day, as Lindsay's – a breathy, alto voice that was pleasant on the ears. Lindsay sat down opposite him.

"So," she said. "Ralsty dragged you out to meet your audience, eh?"

Grant looked at Lindsay's face – a pleasant diversion. She looked to be in her late 30s or early 40s, and she carried herself well, with a trim body inside of her black dress and a cheery, friendly, well-proportioned face.

"Are you having fun observing all of us?" Lindsay said. She took a sip of her wine, then licked its aftertaste from her lips. She had abandoned her lipstick.

"I'm not used to carrying on a conversation by myself," Lindsay said. Her voice was the only one Grant heard in the room, as though his own silence had helped him develop an ability to discard the noise of others, to focus on a single voice or musical note in a mural of sound.

"You have an intense stare," Lindsay said, blinking, then returning Grant's gaze. "It could be intimidating, if someone let it. But I won't let it." She smiled, the kind of smile that was more than a casual grin offered to a stranger.

Lindsay leaned forward and was practically whispering now, but Grant heard her voice louder than the Doobie Brothers on the speakers and the boisterous laughter that broke out at the bar, louder than Ralston's voice somewhere around him, perhaps in the booth behind him, telling someone about the task of plotting his novel, which was after all more important in his life and in the greater scheme of writing than any piece of investigative journalistic tripe could be.

"I'd love to know what's inside that head of yours," Lindsay said. "I'll bet you have some damned interesting thoughts. You must, with the kind of pictures you take. Those aren't the photographs of a shallow thinker."

Grant took a long drink of beer as he listened to Lindsay, as though the two of them had the bar to themselves. He stared at her face as she talked, at the way her lips parted slightly, just enough to let the words out, at how she didn't just sip the wine but let it linger on her tongue, against her cheeks, before swallowing it, at the way her hair stopped just even with the bottom of her jaw, almost a negative opposite of his wife's black hairstyle. When she blinked her eyes, it was a slow, almost deliberate blink, like she wanted to savor the sight she was briefly closing out.

"My but you stare," Lindsay said. "Is that the photographer in you, or do you find me interesting? No answer necessary."

Ralston scooted into the booth next to Grant. "Hey pal, you ready for another one? I think I'm going to head out before long." Ralston looked at Grant, then at Lindsay, at the stares they were sharing. "Oh," he said like a kid who'd wandered in on his parents in bed. "Excuse me. About a half hour, OK Grant?"

Ralston stood up and left the two alone in the booth.

"Looks like you have to be leaving," Lindsay said. "I'd ask you to give me a ring, but it looks like you already have one." She glanced at his left hand.

Lindsay picked up her wine glass, took a

long last drink, then set it down and moved to the end of the booth. She was about to stand up, then looked into Grant's face again.

"You ever do nudes?" Lindsay giggled. "No, I didn't say news. Nudes. Naked women."

She leaned forward, whispering again. "I've always wanted to do a nude shoot. I've never met a photographer who interested me enough, or who I would let do it. You certainly wouldn't shoot and tell, would you? I wonder if you'd be interested, if you'd let me pose for you one day."

Grant returned Lindsay's gaze.

"I'll be in touch," Lindsay said. She stood up and started to walk away, then stopped, turned, and gave Grant one last look. The bottles of liquor glistened on the bar behind her, the light of the bar backlit her, outlining the curves of her body in its black dress with the white leg poking out of its slit; she posed for a moment for Grant, then dissolved into the crowd.

Grant drank the last of the beer in his bottle, glanced toward the door, saw Ralston engaged in a conversation. He went to the bar for one more refill. He handed the empty to the bartender and waited for a fresh drink.

"Hey," said a voice next to him. "You're the newspaper photographer. I was at your show today."

Grant looked toward the voice, saw a man looking at him. The man had a fat face, a sparse, black moustache, brown-frame glasses, black hair that was mussy like he'd just gotten out of bed.

"Hell of a set of pictures," the man said. "I'm a bit of a camera nut myself. I was looking for you at the exhibit today, but some asshole at the bar decided I'm the guy he wanted to tell his life story to. You know how that goes."

Grant looked at the man, listening to him. He wore a pair of blue jeans, brown leather sandals, a collared sport shirt that strove to contain a belly that spilled over his pants waist.

"So how long it take you to do that photo essay?" the man said. "Let me get that drink." He took a couple of bills out of his pants pocket and handed them to the barman.

"Name's Todd," the man said, extending the hand that wasn't holding a bottle of beer.

Grant took the hand, and Todd held on with a firm, lingering shake.

"Yours is Grady, right? Grady Barker, right?" Todd continued to shake Grant's hand up and down.

"Listen," Todd said. "There a reason you're

not answering me?"

Jimmy Morrison sang on the speakers all around Grant. The din, the yakking and laughing and yelling of the bar, filled his ears. He could barely hear Todd, who finally let his hand drop. Grant picked up his new beer and began drinking it, glancing beyond Todd's shoulder for Ralston. He saw the reporter smiling, pushing through folks, moving toward Grant.

"What?" Todd said, raising his voice. "I bought you a drink. Least you can do is talk to me. I just wanna talk cameras, OK? I'm not gonna pry into your personal business, that blonde little number you were talking to over there. What, you too good to talk to me? Fucking artist? That it?"

Grant set his beer bottle on the bar and started to back away. Todd moved forward, his gaze intent on Grant.

"Goddam it, I'm talking to you," Todd said, his face reddening. "What'd I do, insult you by buying you a goddam drink and complimenting your pictures?"

Suddenly Grant was in the middle of a circle with Todd, like a couple of boxers in a ring. Todd was closing in on him; the whole place was quiet except for an acoustic guitar strumming on the speakers, a succession of slow, melodic chords.

Todd stopped, looked around him at the faces, rows and rows of faces staring at him and Grant.

"Asshole's too good to fuckin' talk to me," Todd said, his head moving from face to face in the bar. Then he looked back at Grant. "I'm gonna kick his snobbish ass out onto the street."

Then, a flash of black, a splash of liquid; Todd stood facing Grant with wine dripping from his face.

"You're a belligerent, obnoxious drunk," Lindsay said, stepping between Grant and Todd, holding her empty wine glass. Todd froze, his face wet with Lindsay's wine. Ralston stepped out of the circle; the reporter grasped Grant by the arm and pulled him toward the front door. The mass of drinkers parted, making an aisle on the tiled floor, a safe passage for Ralston and Grant to tread as they made their way to the street, then converging again, blocking Todd from following.

But the drunk remained rigid, his face red, as he stared at Lindsay. She then jerked her head away from him, tossing her blonde hair, and she walked into the crowd, then to the bar.

"I'll have another wine," she said to the man behind the bar. "And he's paying for it."

Todd went to the bar, took out his wallet, laid a ten dollar bill on the dark, polished wooden counter, then pocketed his wallet like an Old West gunslinger putting away his piece, and he walked out of the bar into the city night – looking, vainly, for one quiet photographer who'd made a hasty escape.

XI

Seeing her sitting there unresponsive makes me realize that silence has a sound.

— Jodi Picoult, My Sister's Keeper

Clevenger leaned back in his seat at the desk, opposite Grant. He folded his hands together behind his neck and used them for a neck rest. His eyes were closed.

"Y'know, Grant, they say there is a good woman behind every successful man. But I've got a variation on that theme. I say there is a father behind every successful man."

The psychiatrist grinned.

"I wanted to be a piano player when I was a kid," he said. "I know that might seem strange. Most parents pull their teeth out trying to get their kids to practice musical instruments. But my father couldn't keep me away from the piano. After school, when the other kids were playing ball, I'd be at the piano working the keyboard. My father thought I was weird. He couldn't understand my lack of interest in athletics. He'd take me outside to throw a baseball or football around – man, when it came to sports, I was all thumbs. But when it came to the keyboard, my fingers were graceful. My piano teacher, whom my father paid for grudgingly, told me I had a natural talent. He was an old jazz player around town, had his own combo that played at the Elks on Saturday nights. He gave me a record once, Lennie Tristano. Man, I took that thing home and played it and played it until my father finally threatened to break it – so I waited until he was gone, or while he was at work, and played it some more."

Clevenger stopped talking for a bit. He kept his eyes closed, remembering his piano, his father. His head leaning back accentuated his Adam's apple, which was still now, as he thought. His mouth formed into a slight frown.

"He finally wore me down. Or maybe I saw the light. Music's a tough life, a hard career. Most people can't make a living at it; and those that do, well, like my old man said, the hours are awful, or you're on the road most of your life. So I went to college and studied psychology, and today I'm a successful head shrinker. I have a nice house, a nice family, a good retirement account, I've got one kid in college planning to study law, another in her last year of high school, wants to be a teacher. My wife and I go to Europe once a year. We have a lodge in the hills. So I've done alright, and I have my collection of piano players on CD at home. Music's a wonderful hobby, like my father said it would be. Not much time to listen to them, though."

The psychiatrist sat up straight, resting his arms on his lap.

"Hell. I even still play sometimes. After my father died, my mother moved to a smaller place. She'd always kept the piano in the living room, said it reminded her of me as a kid. But when she moved, she gave it to me. I put it in my living room. Sometimes, after my wife's gone to bed, when I'm sitting up at night, can't sleep, maybe having a drink and listening to music, I go sit down at the piano. I still know some of the old stuff by heart."

The doctor gazed backward in time; his face tightened for a moment. "The thing is, I wonder how good I might have been, how much I might enjoy my life now, if that son of a bitch hadn't stopped me."

Clevenger sighed and looked at Grant. "I think I could have been good. Maybe not as good as I am at what I do now. But good enough. I won-der sometimes what direction my life might have taken had I pursued playing the piano. It's good sometimes, Grant, to fantasize about your life, to think about what might have been. It helps you maintain your perspective; if you're happy with what you do, it helps you to appreciate it. But it's also healthy to tap into your past, to revisit old dreams. Who knows. I might even start practicing the piano again, maybe put together a little combo just to screw around, like a hobby, y'know. Some people garden. I can put together the Matt Clevenger Trio and do weddings like you shoot your pictures on the side – the pictures that matter most to you, right? Speaking of which, I saw in the paper that some of your work is on display at the newspaper. I've been meaning to get over there and take a look at it. Looks like you're doing OK. I do think our sessions are doing you some good. Your face seems more expressive, at least – it won't surprise me if you come in here and talk my leg off one day. Your work plan pays for a total of ten sessions, and you've used five, so I see no reason to stop them. Do you want to continue your sessions?"

Grant nodded.

"I don't suppose you're ready to write down anything for me."

Grant stared at the doctor.

"That's fine. I'll continue to consult with colleagues. I'll continue to research. But other than the silence you subject those around you to, I really am not overly concerned about you, Grant. Not when you're holding down your job, living in a successful marriage, putting your work on public display. I'll see you here next time, then."

The doctor stood up, cuing Grant that the hour was over. Grant went to the door and gently pulled it shut behind him. The receptionist smiled at him as she handed him a card with the date and time of the next appointment.

In his car, Grant put Stan Getz into his CD player. Getz's breathy Latin jazz and the car's air conditioning blew through the interior as he drove to work. He sat in the parking lot of the newspaper for a few minutes, listening to the clean drum stick strokes on the ride cymbal as Getz explored a melody, to the buzz of the bass – he pictured Dr. Clevenger at a piano, wearing slacks, a black turtleneck beneath which his Adam's apple moved up and down in time to the music as the psychiatrist bobbed his head back and forth to a jazz tune he performed on the piano.

The Matt Clevenger Theory of Fathers and the Matt Clevenger Trio, the soul of a shrink and a musician in the same body – now there might be an interesting face to photograph up close, the detailed expressions of an analytical mind exploring the improvisational world of jazz, logic meeting emotion at the corner of C sharp and D.

A group of reporters were gathered at Ralston's desk when Grant walked into the office.

"Hey Grant!" Ralston waved at the photographer, motioning for him to come to the gathering.

"The Metro's done it again," Ralston said, holding up a copy of the weekly alternative newspaper. On the front was a color photograph of an Hispanic man standing in front of the Riverton turkey plant, with the Spanish words superimposed over it in stark, white lettering: Que Pasa?"

"I'll tell you what's happening," Ralston said, answering the question for the gathering of reporters, editors and photographers. "We're seeing a smear job by a sloppy third-rate ad sheet that claims to be a second option in print journalism. Listen to this."

Ralston opened the tabloid newspaper to an inside page, under the headline: Responsible Journalism Goes South. It was bylined by Ray MacDonald.

"In its latest entry into this year's state Associated Press investigative reporting category, the Bulletin has put forth an admirable, in-depth piece of reporting by would-be novelist B. Sinclair Ralston that takes a look at the socio-economic conditions of the children of the labor force of the Bingham Farms turkey farm north of town – and surprise, surprise, the newspaper has discovered less-than-ideal living conditions, a community barely getting by with sub-poverty and sub-standard wages and housing. Ralston has brought out – drum roll, please – learned university professors and social scientists, who properly and correctly point out that these immigrant, migrant workers are struggling to educate their children, to feed and house them and to fend off sickness and disease.

"John Steinbeck, where are you when we need you?" the article continued, as read in Ralston's booming voice. "The Bulletin is making rancid wine of 'The Grapes of Wrath.' Ralston, lackey to Bulletin editor Derek Fisher who is a pillar of this city's white community, member in good standing at the country club, vice president of the Rotary Club, has struck with the blinding sword of liberalism. Fisher has demonstrated that his normally right-wing newspaper can left-wing it with the best of us in this unabashed, slanted piece of would-be reporting apparently designed

THE SILENT TREATMENT

to mend this city's largest newspaper's lower-class fences."

"Whew," said Tracy, standing next to Ralson, reading over his shoulder.

"There's more," Ralston said. He read on:

"As it stands, this Journalism 101 exercise in skewering corporate America succeeds at painting a verbal picture of a big company exploiting the lower classes, at presenting an industrial example of the economic slavery that today's American economy, which relies more and more on the world's lower classes for its production process, has become. But the Bulletin series' strength – this picture of corporate greed as presented in the articles – is just that. A picture – a snapshot of financial Americana. It doesn't tell the whole story.

"For example," Ralston continued reading to his quiet audience, "it does not touch upon the economic usury rampant in the city proper. No, this series of articles goes north, to a separate village that is indeed little more than a company town – leaving untouched the huge companies that comprise this city's economic base and the low wage scales, that advertise in the pages of the Bulletin, the union-busting, the increasing pressure to maintain a growing bottom line at the expense of the workers' benefits, pay and dignity. And of course, nowhere will you find discussed in this article the wage and benefit structure, the low morale, the exploitation of the workers at the Bulletin – workers with whom the Metro compete in journalistic endeavors but who share the Metro's goal of thorough, investigative and honest journalism."

Ralston laid the newspaper on his desk. He grinned at the gathering.

"And so on," he said. "They quote their own experts, union bosses, university professors who have a bone to pick with the Bulletin, all of them tearing us apart because we didn't take on the whole goddam corporate structure of the city. Bunch of goddam garbage."

Ralston pulled at his chin with his long, pale fingers.

"Thing is," he said, "they obviously knew what was going to be in my series before it came out. They needed at least a week to throw together the kind of research they did for this crap. They couldn't have put their piece together so fast otherwise. Somebody's been talking to them, somebody who knew what we were doing has gone to them and told them all about it."

He glanced around the room, stopping his

gaze at Grant, grinned and shook his head no. "Couldn't be you."

The reporters began to disperse, returning to their desks. Grant went to Ralston's desk and looked at the copy of the Metro that Ralston had dropped there.

"Take it," Ralston said. "I've read all of it – nothing worth looking at in that piece of shit excuse for a newspaper. The thing that irks me is you see this pseudo publication in people's hands at the clubs, at the restaurants. They eat this shit up – this so-called article that's really nothing more than a long editorial diatribe against our good work, that doesn't dispute one fact put forth in our newspaper but that uses questionable sources just to drag us down. I hate these bastards. I hope I run into MacDonald at the Club Cafe one of these nights. I'm gonna buy that son of a bitch a beer just for the pleasure of throwing it in his goddam face."

Grant picked up the newspaper and carried it to the photo department. He sat down in a chair a few feet from Walt's desk.

"What'd he expect?" Walt said, motioning with his hand toward Ralston. "If he expects the alternative press to sing his praises like everyone around here does, he's living in a fictional world."

Grant sat in the chair and leafed through the Metro, eyeing the ads for the city's nightclubs and restaurants, the entertainment listings. He thumbed past some movie reviews, a restaurant review, a couple of pages of CD reviews. He stopped on page 16, Lindsay Cameron's column on the arts, "For Art's Sake."

The first several paragraphs were devoted to a new art gallery, called The Third Eye, located in the neighborhood of the Club Cafe. The article contained a few quotes from the gallery's owner, a transplanted Californian who said he hoped to bring some fresh artistic perspectives to the city. New blood enlivens and revitalizes a place, he said, telling Lindsay that his gallery would seek out innovative work not only of the local artists but of regional and national artists as well. He planned to establish a base of artists in his shop but also to bring in visiting exhibits of work that he promised would be fresh, exciting and avant-garde. The photograph with the article showed the owner, who wore a bandana, a couple of gold earrings and a pencil-thin moustache straight out of a 1940s black-and-white movie, posing in the middle of an ornate, wide, empty brown wooden frame.

Then Grant got to the last few paragraphs,

where he saw his name.

"I got the chance to stop in at the Bulletin's new front lobby exhibit of photographer Grant Baker's work over the weekend," Lindsay wrote, "and was more than pleasantly surprised to find a photographic display that is fresh and vital and that demonstrates the best artistic attributes of photography. A surprising aspect of the display – and of the work accompanying B. Sinclair Ralston's recent Bulletin series on immigrant workers – is its reliance on black-and-white photography. The strengths of black-and-white images have been largely ignored by newspapers, and thus by photographers in general, since front pages became rainbows of graphics and largely throw-away cutesy color feature photos of children playing or artisans creating their baubles and pots. The photographs in this exhibit and in this series explore the possibilities of contrast, the uses of focus and perspective, the old technique of framing scenes with natural elements such as tree trunks or lamp posts."

Walt stood up. "I'm going outside to have a smoke in the great outdoors," he said. He glanced over Grant's shoulder as the photographer read Lindsay's column.

"I wondered how long it would take you

to find that piece," Walt said as he moved toward the door. "Of writing, I mean."

Grant looked up, saw Walt's back side going through the door toward the newsroom exit and the sunshiny back lawn that bordered the parking lot. He went back to Lindsay's column.

"Baker's exhibit speaks to us from an artistic depth – and his is work that will have to be taken at face value. The photographer is mute, so there was no opportunity to discuss with him his intentions or his techniques. Suffice to say, this shooter lets his work speak for him, and it speaks volumes. What you see in the image is what you get – and it is more than enough. Baker's pictures of the workers and their families – especially those focusing on the faces – stand as testament to a community of workers, wives, fathers and children, who labor hard, who live hard and who love hard. The photographer uses shadows and shading, light and depth of field to portray depth of soul – and despair. This is a truly rare instance of newspaper photography as art; and I can only hope that Baker has other projects on his photographic easel."

The article included a boxed paragraph of information about the newspaper show, its address and hours of operation. Grant laid the newspaper on his lap, glancing down at it now and then. After a few minutes, he picked it up, folded it and put it into his camera bag, in a side compartment, to take home for Pauline to read.

Walt came back in.

"How much booze you buy her at the Club Cafe that night?" Walt said. He grinned. "That was really quite a writeup. I doubt the glassholes will notice it – not considering the front-page piece in this edition. But I'll bring it to their attention, when the time is better. Fisher's in a mood today. I'm sure he's seen the Metro piece, and I'm sure we'll get an earful of it at today's budget meeting. Personally, I think we give too much credit and attention to the Metro – I mean, our own staff grabs it off the stands the minute it comes out. The guy who wrote the piece slamming our series applied to work here once and Fisher showed him the door pretty quickly. But don't think that Mr. MacDonald wouldn't drop his anti-Bulletin facade in a second if Derek Fisher invited him down for a job interview. Anyway, looks like you and Lindsay Cameron certainly found a meeting of the minds."

Walt went back to his desk, got onto his computer and began ordering printouts of the photos he had on hand to offer at that afternoon's budget meeting. He gave Grant an assignment to get on the way home, a color shoot of a backyard and flower garden that would be in a features section spread on an upcoming home and garden tour sponsored by the chamber of commerce and the city's garden club.

At home, Grant put a Herbie Mann CD on the stereo. Mann's soft, jazzy flute filled the room as Grant read again through Lindsay's column. He leaned his head back, listened to the raspy snare drum, the brushes sliding across the tight skin, to Mann's mellow horn; he pictured the Bulletin's lobby, his photographs on display, the people gathering in front of his pictures, pointing out certain details in each one, discussing his work as though, even for a moment at least, it actually had some meaning.

The telephone rang. Grant sat up, started to his feet, then stopped. He leaned back into the couch and listened as the answering machine picked up the call.

"This is Andrew Bowman, director of the city's ArtScape program, telephoning for Grant Baker," the voice said on the answering machine. "Mr. Baker, I just read Lindsay Cameron's piece in the Metro. I have seen the display of photographs she wrote about, and I agree with her on its merits. An exhibit planned for our East Side gallery has fallen through, and I'm wondering if you might be interested in showing some of your work at that gallery. Please give me a call at your convenience to discuss this."

The caller left a telephone number. Grant sat in the couch and replayed the message in his mind a couple of times, then let his mind wander idly, along with Herbie Mann's flute, among the wonderful possibilities and meanderings of one's life.

Like the contrast in a photograph of a white field of fresh snow beneath a black, starless night sky, Ralston's lousy day had been Grant's good day.

XII

In human intercourse the tragedy begins, not when there is misunderstanding about words, but when silence is not understood.

– Henry David Thoreau

Grant stood on the sidewalk opposite Lindsay's apartment. Her place was on the second floor of a two-story commercial building complex. The building, a stack of sooty red brick, was in the Club Cafe area of the city, about five blocks away from the bar – just at the lower rent edge of the transition zone from the Club Cafe neighborhood to the old buildings and houses that had not yet been claimed by the city's young architects and developers. Below her, a tavern claimed one corner; country music played on its jukebox, barely audible on the street among the noise of the passing cars. Next to the tavern sat a shoe repair shop, closed for the night, and then an empty store front that carried a big white For Lease sign in red paint in its front window.

The photographer studied Lindsay's apartment – she had told him that hers was the south-ernmost four windows looking down on the street above the vacant store front. She had phoned him at work; Walt took the call, handed the telephone to Grant at her request. She told Grant she was still interested in the nude photo shoot if he was so inclined. That was how she put it in her voice, which was soft and low over the telephone.

"I'll plan on you dropping by about seven or so, if you're so inclined," she said. "That way, we can take advantage of the evening sunlight, which I've always found to be exquisite."

Grant listened on the phone as Walt watched from behind his desk. Grant gave no indication to Walt that the woman on the other end was offering to take her clothes off and pose for him. He listened to her instructions, then hung up the telephone.

"You get what you needed out of that conversation?" Walt said.

Grant nodded, then grabbed his camera bag – the newspaper had sprung for a new 35-mil-limeter film camera for him after his last one was smashed – and left for his afternoon assignments.

Pauline asked few questions when he left the house. Her usual: "For the paper or for you?"

Grant pointed to himself.

Pauline read the day's newspaper as a can of soup warmed on the stove. "For God's sake, try to stay out of trouble. Anybody bothers you, just take that sign out of your pocket that I made you. Show it to them for God's sake so they know you can't talk, OK?"

Grant stopped at the door. He smiled at Pauline. She got up from the table, walked over to him. She hugged him.

"Y'know, you and I are communicating better than we ever have. Isn't that amazing? Please, Grant, be careful."

He nodded to Pauline, returned her hug, then went out the door.

Grant saw a shadow pass across the drawn shade in Lindsay's apartment window second from the right. The shadow stopped, bent over as though retrieving something from the floor, then stood straight again. It shook its head quickly, as though drying itself off from the shower. Grant had always been intrigued by windows in houses, in apartments. He sometimes stared at them for several minutes during his walks, or while waiting at stop signs or traffic lights. He tried to imagine the lives that were being lived behind them – multi-paned windows of upstairs bedrooms; picture windows glistening clean in front of thick, drawn drapes; second-story windows with painted shutters; attic windows that were dark and secretive; hundreds of windows in tall brick apartment buildings, some of them lit up at night so that at a distance the side of the building looked like an electric crossword puzzle grid.

Someday he wanted to do a series of photographs of windows, to let the windows tell the stories of their owners – dark windows with delicate lace curtains at their sides; upstairs apartment windows with yellow light glowing behind drawn, thin shades; dining room windows with chandeliers blazing beyond elegant draperies; stained windows covered by soiled bed sheets.

Staring at the city's windows, Grant imagined sweating lovers entwined on white sheets in a four-poster mahogany bed behind dusty white blinds; an old woman sitting in an easy chair behind a TV tray sipping on hot tea as she watched her favorite evening quiz program amid built-in oak bookcases and a blue carpet with a pink flower pattern; a student sitting at a desk, his sleeping head resting on top of an open book with a chart illustrating percentages of corn and soybean production in comparison to the nation's total agricultural output as a yellow lamp shone down on his hair; a couple sitting in a parlor in front of a simmering fireplace, him sipping a martini, she a vodka tonic, as the evening sun prisms through a leaded glass window next to a solid oak door; a young couple preparing for a night at the symphony behind the lace curtains of an upstairs bedroom – he pulling on a pair of dark slacks beneath a T-shirt pulled over bulging muscles while she was in the bathroom showering, her naked body almost perceptible behind the dimpled shower door. Grant imagined the photographs of the lives being lived behind the thousands, millions of city windows, the joy, the anxiety, the terror, the anticipation, the nerves, the sadness – heads in windows, eyes bright and eager, lips thick and pouting, cheeks smudged with tears, foreheads marked by grit, ears displaying sparkling diamonds, noses pockmarked and reddened from decades of cheap whiskey, moustaches, pimples, rouge, thick eyelashes, goatees, silver teeth that glisten in the glare of a camera flash, deep, soulful eyes that know, that understand, that forgive.

The elation and despair of a universe can be found in a single face – and therefore in a single photograph.

Lindsay answered her door wearing a pink

terry cloth robe tied at the waist. She wore no makeup; her hair was freshly showered and blow-dried.

She smiled as she pulled the door open.

"So, you've come," she said. "I thought you might. Of course, it was hard to tell. It's hard to set this sort of thing up with a man who can't speak if you hope to keep it secret – and I do hope to keep this secret. Between you and me. Agreed?"

Grant nodded. He entered the doorway and walked into a living room with a high, white ceiling above a set of crystal glass lit up by bulbs hanging down from its center.

"You brought the film camera, not the digital, like I asked?" Again, Grant nodded.

"I'll be right back." Lindsay went through a swinging wooden door into the next room. Grant put his camera case and tripod on the floor, then sat down in an easy chair with a blue slip cover in a corner next to the front door. On the opposite wall stood a tall wooden bookcase filled mostly with hardback volumes. Paintings and photographs – abstract balls of color floating on white canvas like lost balloons; charcoal figures of men and women with deep eye sockets and long, narrow faces; more colored balls, these like floating Christmas tree ornaments; historical photographs of downtown buildings and bridges – covered the clean, white walls of the room – walls that ended at a dark, wooden floor that was covered with a large, blue oval throw rug that had smudges of white in it like giant crayon marks. It was the apartment of an artist.

Lindsay pushed through the swinging door carrying a glass of white wine and a bottle of light beer. She handed the beer to Grant.

"I believe that's the brand I saw you drinking at the Club Cafe the other evening," she said.

Grant nodded.

"You do communicate." Lindsay smiled and gave Grant a friendly wink of her lovely blue right eye. She sat on a stool in the middle of the room, then noticed Grant observing the paintings on the walls.

"All mine, except the photographs," she said. "In various stages of my apprenticeship as an artist. I've been painting for almost twenty years under a number of teachers – but I still think I'm an apprentice. I haven't found my voice yet, as a writer would say – my milieu, I suppose." She grinned again and took a drink of wine and then another.

"I guess I'm just a bit nervous," she said, her glass of wine nearly gone already. "I mean, I've posed in the buff before. I'm no novice. Back in art school. Our model didn't show up one night, so I volunteered. Made an easy twenty bucks and bought drinks for my classmates afterwards."

She looked Grant in the eyes. "It's strictly artistic. Nothing sexual about it. I mean, of course artists have made lovers of their models – happens all the time. But the act itself – the painting, the picture taking – there's nothing sexual about that. The artist is like a doctor, that's all; the doctor looks at the muscles, at the skin, checks for bruises, abrasions, whatever. The artist studies the form, the shadows, the crevices, the bumps – the artist tries to depict the image not just in a realistic way but, in the best rendering of a nude study, manages to find more. A smirk. A certain look in the eye. The way the model might carry the body. Different artists will see different bodies in different ways. One might render an obese model as an ugly wharf monster, the next imaging her as a mountain nymph. We each of us bring our own attitudes to the subject – as I'm sure you realize as a photographer. The way you use your focus, or select a lens or a filter, the lighting – all set a mood, shed a certain kind of light on your subject."

Lindsay smiled again, got down from

the stool. "I'm lecturing, aren't I? I teach a night course at the city university, you know, just basic life drawing 101. And I teach a course in journalistic writing – critical writing – at the community college. I need one more wine, then I think I'll be ready. Another beer?"

Grant shook his head no.

"Good," Lindsay said, pushing through the door that led to the kitchen. "We're having a downright conversation tonight."

She returned moments later with a glass filled to the lip with white wine and a fresh beer for Grant.

"You don't have to drink it, but it's there if you want it."

Lindsay sat again on the stool.

"The lighting is how I like it," Lindsay said. She undid her robe and let it drop to the floor. She sat on the stool in the middle of her apartment naked as a Mexican Chihuahua – the only hair she had was on her head. Grant stared for a moment at her body, the breasts that were firm, with wide, dark aureolas and small nipples, the stomach that curved out slightly, suggesting the pinkish belly of a Rubens painting, the bald crotch cradled between white thighs that sloped down to shapely calves and then feet that ended in toenails painted pink. It was a lovely body.

Lindsay grinned. "I do hope that is the stare of an artist and not of a horny man," she said, her face pale. She was totally unembarrassed.

Grant took his 35-millimeter from the camera bag. He opened his tripod and mounted the camera, focusing on Lindsay, who sat in a wide splash of evening sunlight that poured into the window, reflected from the glass front of the building across the street. Lindsay's body cast a long, black shadow behind her. Grant began shooting as Lindsay sat, altering her pose slightly as the photographer moved from side to side, dragging his tripod, adjusting his focus, moving forward, backward, replacing spools of film as he shot – she crossed her legs, she covered her crotch with her folded arms, she held her arms behind her head, her chest thrust out.

Grant changed to the zoom lens, moved in on Lindsay's face. He shot extreme closeups of lips, firm cheeks, a long, sloping nose.

"I need more wine," Lindsay said as Grant stood up and stepped back from the camera, eyeing Lindsay, considering different angles. "And you haven't touched your beer."

She got down from the stool. Grant listened to the padding of her feet as they stepped off the carpet and onto the floor, then went through the door onto the black and white checkered tile of the next room. He went to the easy chair, picked up his bottle of beer and took a couple of long drinks, draining the first bottle. He grabbed the second, took another drink.

"Thirsty?" Lindsay said, carrying her glass of wine from the kitchen. The cloudy, white liquor caught the fading red of the sun so that Lindsay was carrying a dripping wet ray of light in her hand. She stood in front of Grant for a moment; his eyes followed the curve of her body from the shoulders to the thin waist, back out over the hips and then gently sloping inward again to the feet.

Lindsay climbed back onto her stool. Dusk began filtering into the room, darkening it slightly, as the final rays of that day's sun fell away. The two of them sat quietly for a few minutes, each sipping their drinks. Grant opened his camera and deposited a fresh roll of film.

"Y'know, I didn't have anything to do with that cover piece on your newspaper's stories," Lindsay said. "I know its author; we've had a few drinks at the Club Cafe. He's just your typical reporter – full of himself, eager, wants to make his mark. I disagree with what he wrote."

Grant leaned back in his chair and listened to Lindsay.

"I just wanted you to know that. I just write a weekly column for them, they give me a paycheck, they give me a free dinner now and then on one of their advertising tradeouts with restaurants. It's just part of how I make my living until I, you know, paint that one work or series that establishes me, until I can make my living from art. Though I doubt I'll ever stop writing about it; I like the writing process, the putting of words on paper, or on the screen. It's a different kind of creativity than painting, with different challenges – you know, putting images into people's heads by creating scenes with words, by describing things, instead of by showing them with drawings or paintings. But I'm a painter first and last."

As Lindsay talked, Grant stood up with his camera. He watched her through its lens, watched her lips move. He lay on the floor in front of her and shot up toward her head, framing her face with her legs. He got onto his knees and focused now on her belly, its curve down into her thighs. He moved to her side and shot her arms and torso and limbs as ivory, shadowed slopes in the darkening apartment. He shot without a flash, wanting to preserve and accentuate the soft dusk shadows instead of photographing the dark, stark shadows that a flash would produce.

He moved to her front and, standing, focused sharply on her face, moving closer.

"I can see your eyes through the lens," Lindsay said, grinning. "I can see right into you, Grant. I can see your very soul. Ah yes, you do have a soul, there it is now, peering at me, dark and brooding, like your pictures."

Lindsay giggled.

"You're an interesting man, Grant," she said. "An intelligent man. I know that without ever hearing you utter a word. I know that because I know you, Grant. You're like me."

Grant moved closer, concentrating on Lindsay's eyes, two pools of blue with a clear island of round blackness in the middle. He looked through the lens into her right pupil, into the dark interior of Lindsay – into a void.

"You're frustrated. You despair." Lindsay's voice was all around Grant. "You're like John Lennon's fool on the hill, you look around you in your silence, you listen to and watch the rest of the silly world go by, and what you see depresses you. It's all so hopeless and meaningless.

I know that about you, Grant, because I can see it in your pictures, I can see it in your eyes – and it's what I see in the world, too."

Grant moved backward, still looking through his lens, though he was finished photographing naked Lindsay. He focused from blur to soft to sharp; he stood and watched Lindsay. She stared straight through the lens into his eyes. He put down the camera, let it hang from his neck.

Lindsay stood up, grabbed her robe and wrapped it around her. It was soft, like her face. She smiled and stepped toward Grant. Her lips came toward him, he let them. Her mouth came to his and Lindsay kissed him, gently pushing her sweet tongue against his lips, then into his mouth. Then she stepped back, picked up her wine and took a long drink.

"Let's just sit here and drink our drinks," she said.

Grant sat down in the chair. Lindsay returned to the stool. The robe fell slightly away from her legs, revealing her upper left thigh. The robe was loose below her neck, exposing the top of her breasts. She looked erotic, half naked in her robe, her short hair mussed, natural, her eyes wide as she studied Grant.

"I want all of the rolls of film, Grant," she

said. "I'll have a friend develop them for me. I have a hundred dollar bill for you, for your film, your time and your work. These pictures are for nobody but me. I plan to use them to do a self portrait, a self-portrait nude."

Grant picked up the used rolls of film from the floor. He stood up and carried them to a desk that was between the door and a wall, at a window looking out onto the neighborhood. Night had fallen; car headlights poked up and down the avenue below. People walked the sidewalks.

"Wait here," Lindsay said, standing up. "I'll get your money and each of us another drink. It's early yet. We have time for our drinks and to watch the night."

Lindsay went through the swinging door, toward, Grant guessed, the kitchen and then the bedroom beyond that. He collapsed his tripod, put his camera and lenses into his bag, then he stood up and quietly let himself out the door. His camera still contained the film of Lindsay's face, the closeups he had taken at the last – pictures he wanted, that he knew she wouldn't miss, that he considered a fair trade for a hundred dollars.

He hustled down the stairs to the street, put his gear into the trunk of his car. He sat behind the wheel for a moment, watching Lindsay's apartment. He saw her shadow cross the room farthest to the right, then the light there flickered off. The shadow moved across the window shade of the next room, then he saw her standing in her living room, from the waist up, in her pink robe. She held a glass of fresh wine in her hand. Her head moved from side to side as she looked around the empty room. Grant started his car and drove away.

He parked down the street from the Club Cafe. He exited the car, walked along the sidewalk, listening to the sound of his footsteps on the cement. Inside the place, which was half full on this week night, he went to the bar, pointed to the tap, indicating a light beer. He paid the bartender and carried his glass of cold, foaming beer to an empty booth. He sat there for nearly an hour, listening to the juke box, to the small, quiet conversations, the laughter in the place, watching the drinkers sit at the bar, watching the television flicker above them, the sound low, actors on the small screen moving out of sequence to the rhythm of the music coming from the speakers, an electric guitar, Eric Clapton playing a blues riff.

Then, a young woman, maybe old enough to drink, maybe not, her shoulder-length dark hair stringy, parted down the middle, sat down across from him.

"Kind of a quiet night," she said. "Mind if I join you?"

Grant voiced no objection.

"I'm not lookin' for nothin'," the woman said, her voice shaking. She looked straight at Grant, out of deep, sunken eyes, as she spoke. "I just don't feel like being by myself. But I want to be left alone. You understand the difference, between being alone and being left alone?"

Grant nodded.

The waiter, a bald kid with earrings and a studded, whiskered face, brought Grant another beer. Grant pointed to the woman.

"Coffee," she said. "Just coffee. I just want to sit here and drink my coffee. And I don't want you to pay for my coffee. That OK with you?" She looked at Grant. Her eyes were narrow and dark, her cheeks shallow.

Grant nodded again.

The two of them sat in the booth, Grant drinking his beer, the woman watching him, sipping her coffee, smoking cigarettes, as the juke box played.

"Dirty bastard," the woman muttered softly. Her eyes shot a glance at Grant, then quickly darted around the room. She picked up her coffee, took a drink. "Son of a bitch."

Grant sat quietly as the woman carried on her soliloquy.

"Should've kicked his ass out a long time ago," the woman said.

Grant stared into his beer, watched the bubbles rise through the yellow liquid.

"Love. What a goddam farce. Love." She spit the word "love" out of her mouth like tongue lint.

The two of them sat in their booth, she quietly ranting, Grant providing the perfect silent audience.

"What, you don't talk?" She looked at Grant, blew a puff of smoke out of her mouth.

Grant stared back at her.

She shook her head. "I don't blame you. Talk. What good does it do? Hell, everybody talks and nobody says anything. And what good does it do? Goddam planet's going to hell, half the world's hungry, the other half so fucking rich that nothing matters to nobody, they buy what they want, steal what they can't buy, kill or put into jail anybody who disagrees with them or looks different. Christ. It's all fucked up."

Grant took a long drink of beer.

"Yeah. It don't matter what we say, take out to the streets, yell at the world. Nobody'll hear us anyway, and if they do, they won't listen. Nobody listens. So why talk anyway?"

Grant's eyes widened. He looked into her face, nodded. She took a cigarette out of a pack in a back pocket of her soiled blue jeans. "I don't fucking blame you." She grinned. "What is it they say, yeah, silence is golden. I got a lousy old man, who knows if you got an old lady or what, and here we are drinking our coffee and beer, you in your silence, me moaning, neither one of us can do anything about anything. Maybe I will have a glass of wine, long as you're offering."

Grant motioned for the waiter; the woman ordered a glass of Burgundy.

"I like red wine. Any wine's OK, though. Helps you get through the night. Christ, I don't know if I'll even go home tonight. Let him wonder what the hell happened to me. Hell, he don't listen to me neither, y'know? Nobody's listening."

Grant reached across the table, took her hand. She pulled it back, then relaxed, gave his fingers a squeeze. "Yeah. I know. Me too. You want me? You got a place?"

Grant frowned. He pulled back his hand.

"That's OK. You touched me. Long time

since I been touched, y'know? You didn't have to mean anything by it except you touched me. Only time people touch anymore is to hurt someone else."

She shook her head, looked around the room.

"Christ. Religion. That's what's behind it all. I was in the bus station today, go there sometimes, just to watch, to drink some coffee and watch. Guy leaves a newspaper on the bench next to me, I read a story inside. It's about this drug gang down in Mexico, real violent gang, kill people just for a rock, it says the gang leader claims to be a Christian. He makes his gang members read the Bible every day, memorize parts of it. His neighbors, they all love him, he takes care of them. Says what he's doing is God's work. Then he and his gang, they go out and kill people."

She took a breath of air, then a drink. She looked Grant in the eyes. "He fucking cuts off their heads and then walks away. Just like that. In God's name, cuts off their heads, just like the Middle East."

Grant stood up, drank the last of his beer, dropped a twenty dollar bill on the table and walked out of the bar.

She watched him, fingered the bill and

pulled it toward her. "Shit. This'll be good for another drink. Goddam fool anyway, doubt he heard or understood a word I said."

Grant drove home, found Pauline snoring softly in the bed. He undressed and climbed in next to her. He lay on his back, looking up at the ceiling. He closed his eyes, thought about his last image of Lindsay, sitting on the stool, her legs slightly spread beneath the robe, her smooth, pale skin, her eyes intent on his face which she had looked straight into and through that night, piercing him with those blue eyes of hers.

XIII

When little is done, little is said; silence is the mother of truth.

– Benjamin Disraeli

Grant's brother-in-law turned hamburgers on the grill in the yard as Grant sat on the porch swing and watched. A few clouds hung in the blue sky. A breeze blew in from the ocean. As the family sat down at the big table in the dining room, Grant's brother-in-law twisted open a bottle of red wine and went around the table, filling each glass half full.

"A Napa Valley special," William said of the bottle. "A new winery. Amy and I discovered it a couple days ago, before you all arrived. It's quite good."

The large family surrounded a table filled with tossed salad, potato salad, fruit salad, pasta salad, a platter of hamburgers and hot dogs, apple pie, a plateful of cookies, rows of condiments. Cliff lifted his glass, his spectacles sparkling, and offered a toast.

"To our family," said Cliff, the oldest of the children. His face, like Pauline's, was rectangular and broad. Her whole family was a gathering of wide, muscular blocks, vast chests, big bones. A strong, robust family.

"We're spreading all over the country, but we manage to find each other at least once every year or two," Cliff said. "And that's important."

All raised their glasses and took a sip of wine, then the food began making the rounds.

"I have an announcement," Pauline said.

"Just a minute," her mother said. "Let me finish filling my plate. I like to have all my food on my plate first." She scooped yellow potato salad onto her plate, put mustard and relish on her hamburger bun, then the meat. She forked some tossed salad onto the plate and doused it with orange French dressing.

"OK," she said. "You're pregnant."

The table laughed. Pauline blushed.

"That's all we need," she said. She glanced at Grant, who sat on her left, fixing his hamburger. "Grant's going to show some of his photographs in a gallery."

"Wow," Cliff said. "A real, honest-to-goodness gallery? That's great. But I always did like your work old man. I always said your Christmas snapshots are the best." Cliff chuckled and took a long swig of red wine. "Of course, Christmas pictures and art gallery stuff, that's a bit different. What kind of photos are they?"

"This much I know," Pauline said. "He's gotten out some prints and negatives he wants in the show. Faces."

"Faces," Cliff said. "You mean, like, portraits."

Pauline shook her head. "More than that. Studies of faces. Moods. We just haven't decided which ones yet."

"I guess I'll have to see it," Cliff said.

"That would be wonderful if you could get away for a weekend," Pauline said.

"How long will it be up? Sue's not teaching fall semester."

"Oh, it should still be going then."

Cliff nodded, then turned his attention to the end of the table. "Pass me those hamburger buns, will you pop?"

"Tell me about this gallery," Pauline's mother said. She sat opposite Grant and Pauline. Her gray hair was freshly curled. She wore a pair of tan slacks and a blue blouse. Blue frame glasses perched on her nose. "I don't quite understand art and how it works."

"Well, this weekly newspaper had a piece on some of Grant's work that was on display at his newspaper," Pauline said as she spooned pasta salad onto her plate. "The publisher likes to put art work in his lobby, and sometimes he includes an exhibit of his own photographers' work. It was pictures he took to go along with a series of stories on immigrant workers at a turkey processing plant. This weekly newspaper's arts writer saw it and liked it and wrote about it. Then this gallery guy called and said he wanted to talk to Grant about showing his work."

"I thought Grant couldn't talk," the mother said.

"He can't. I handled it for him."

"My sister the agent," Cliff said, using his wine like water to wash down chewed hamburger. "Way to go, bud."

Grant's mother-in-law took a bite of her hamburger. "Mmmm," she said. "William, the hamburgers are real good. And so's the potato salad Amy."

"What?" Amy said.

"The potato salad's good and so are the hamburgers," William said.

Amy nodded then turned back to her conversation with Sue and Cliff.

It had taken Grant, an only child, a while to get used to being with a large family at holidays. Somehow, they all managed to see each other in person at least every two years.

"Now let me get this straight," Pauline's mother said. "Grant took pictures of people who work at a turkey plant, and the publisher put these pictures on display at the newspaper."

Pauline nodded.

"Pictures of workers."

Pauline nodded again.

"Forgive me Grant," the mother said. "I guess I would have to see them. I've seen some good pictures in our newspaper at home, you know, but I couldn't tell you what makes them good or why I like them. I don't understand art, paintings, either. But I like it. We used to go to the art museum a lot. But no more. We don't go much of anyplace anymore. The mister likes to stay at home most of the time. I guess I do too. We have the television and our programs. We take our walks around the golf course next door."

Grant ate his food and listened to the family noise, the separate conversations scattered around the table, brothers and sisters and wives and husbands chatting about school grades of children, physical maladies of uncles and aunts, the 49ers' prospects in the coming football season, the strange warming trend in the planet's weather patterns, the high cost of apartments and houses in William's and Amy's Marin County neighborhood. It was a loud and loving family; they had adopted Grant, as he had enlisted with them.

After dinner, Grant took his plate of apple pie to the front porch and sat on the swing, looking out over the neighborhood, watching the sidewalks, the yards, listening to the conversations that drifted through the front screen door onto the porch.

His father-in-law pushed through the door. His broad shoulders filled out his white T-shirt, which bulged at his stomach. His body tapered rapidly from the waist down, where baggy gray trousers covered his thin legs. The white socks he wore inside his black loafers matched the white hair that was thin and combed back from a high, broad forehead. He sat in a green plastic porch chair next to Grant.

"That's a nice breeze," he said. "We don't get these in the summer at our place. That's the only part I don't like about New Mexico. The summers. The winters are nice though. We used to like to drive up to Santa Fe, or to the Jemez

Mountains to cool off, but I don't care to drive much anymore. Just to the grocery for some things. We pretty much stay at home the rest of the time. And take our walks. They've got them there swamp coolers in New Mexico, they help keep the house cool."

Grant listened to his father-in-law talk. During past visits, he had asked the old man about his Navy experiences – he'd lied about his age and enlisted as a teenager, seeking to see the world – and about his adventures in the ports of Asia and Europe. Now, without his questions to guide the conversation, Grant simply listened.

"Pauline says you're doing OK," the father said. "I guess it's about your turn to host one of these family visits next summer, ain't it?"

Grant nodded. He looked at the old man's face. It was in pretty good shape for a face that had been through some 80 years. It was full, though the cheeks had begun to sink in a bit. Wrinkles crossed his forehead and crinkled at the corners of his eyes. Skin hung below his neck.

"Y'know, I knew a guy once, he fought in Europe during the second world war. Something happened during the war, just shut him up. He saw doctors. They didn't have a bunch of specialists then, not like they do now. Shell shock.

When I met him, he was working at the plant; we sometimes were in the cafeteria together for lunch. He was always smiling. That's what I remember about him. Never said a word, always smiling. Manny was his name. Smiling Manny."

Grant's mother-in-law came onto the porch.

"You remember that guy I told you about, couldn't talk," the old man said to his wife. "Manny. I told you about him."

She shook her head. "I don't remember. I think I've forgotten half of what you used to tell me when you came home at night. I was busy with the kids then. Now you don't tell me so much."

She smiled at Grant. "You can hear everything all right, huh?"

Grant nodded.

"Dear, Pauline explained it to us," her husband said in a loud voice. "He can hear. He can think. He can work. He just can't talk."

"I know, I know," she said, giving her husband a quick glance that only he, going on 60 years of living with her, could understand clearly. "I'm just making conversation."

The three of them sat quietly for a few minutes.

"I'm gonna get some of that pie," the father-in-law said. He stood up, his skinny legs struggling to lift his upper body. Then he turned and looked Grant in the face.

"Y'know, talkin' ain't all it's cracked up to be. People talk too much today. Politicians. On television. But they got nothin' to say. And us? Nobody listens to you and me anyway, right?"

Then the old man stepped inside the screen door, into the conversational din and laughter of the dining room. Grant heard his wife talking, then Vicki; the two of them laughed in unison as they retold their stories of hanging out in the neighborhood as kids, the boys they liked and didn't like, the girls they envied and despised, the embarrassments and triumphs of their youths.

Grant's mother-in-law looked at him. In turn, he studied her face, which also had weathered the years well – her jaw was firm despite the double, nearly triple, chin. She had rouged her cheeks, and she wore a dark red lipstick. Her eyes were gray and dim.

"Do you mind it so much?" she said. "Not talking?"

Grant shook his head.

"Y'know, it's not so bad. I mean, there are people who lose a leg, people go blind, they lose their hearing. It hurts me to walk. I've got arthritis. I've had triple bypass heart surgery." She smiled. "It's a wonder I'm still around. But I've lived a good life, y'know?"

Grant nodded.

The old lady stood up. "It could have been a lot worse, y'know? A lot worse." She followed her husband's footsteps back into the house, leaving the front porch to Grant.

Listening to the sounds of his wife's family, the television blaring in the living room, the stereo system playing big band hits in the dining room, the chatter and laughter mixing in, Grant recalled the silence of his own home.

On July Fourth, he, his father and mother walked to an ice cream stand down the street, where they bought cones and then went to the lake to watch the fireworks show. They always were at the back of the crowd. Grant's father lifted the boy onto his shoulders, and Grant could see the fireworks exploding in the black sky, the gray smoke drifting in the air, the reflection of the golds and greens and reds and blues and silvers in the shimmering, black water of the lake, where the images of street lights and neon store signs bobbed in the rippling coolness.

They went home then. Grant's father went

inside and sat on the couch, reading the newspaper or a magazine. Grant and his mother sat on the front porch and listened to the neighborhood around them, the pop of the firecrackers back in the alley or up the street, the barking of the neighborhood dogs in response to the firecrackers, the children yelling, the buzz of sparklers in the yard across the street; they twirled them in the air, drawing glowing fire designs on the dark easel of the night.

Christmas morning, Grant's father wore his red and black checkered robe, his brown leather slippers, and he stood over the stove in the kitchen frying eggs and sausage and potatoes. Coarse, dark whiskers covered his chin, jaws and cheeks as Grant's father turned the sausage with a fork, scooped the sliced potatoes with a scallop and flipped them over, stopping to pick up his tan coffee mug and take a sip of hot, black liquid; he put the mug back on the counter next to the stove, and white steam rose out of the cup, mingling with the misty smoke climbing out of the potatos and sausages. The eggs came last, bubbling white with the yellow yolks staring out of the black cast iron skillet like big round eyeballs. Breakfast ready, the three of them sat down at the dining room table. The Christmas tree glowed in the corner, nearly reaching the ceiling, the presents beneath opened and arranged neatly according to owner – a tobacco pouch and sweater for Grant's father, slippers and a sleeping gown for his mother, a transistor radio for listening to baseball games for Grant, along with a couple of new shirts.

Grant didn't like the sausage, but his father insisted that he eat it. He did, then the eggs and a helping of potatoes, washed down with cold, sour orange juice. Afterward, he ran to the bathroom to upchuck the meal, followed by the conversation Grant would always remember, some time or the other, during every Christmas.

"Why did you make him keep eating?" Grant's mother said to his father as Grant lay on the couch, his feet propped up, his face flushed and hot.

"The same reason my father made me eat every meal my mother ever made. You don't waste food. It's a sin."

"Look at him. He's sick. The sausage must have been bad."

"Nah. We ate the sausages. I'm OK. You're OK."

"We're grownups. Our stomachs are stronger. He's just a little boy. He didn't like it.

You made him eat it."

"Well, he's going to be a man someday. It's time he starts learning. He'll be fine and up listening to his new radio in no time."

Grant went in to bed. Later, his mother came in, sat down next to him and gently rubbed his stomach. She put on the table radio, found some Christmas music, then went to the kitchen to clean up the breakfast dishes. Grant lay in bed and listened to the carols as his father sat in the living room, thumbing through the newspaper.

Now, years later, Grant still despised link sausage.

"What's up?" It was David's voice. Grant's son stepped onto the porch and sat down in the green chair where his grandfather had sat before.

"Good food, huh?" David said. He had his mother's wide forehead, her dark hair, his own deep-set, dark eyes. He had sprouted a set of whiskers above his lip that could, if the boy wished, turn into a moustache. His legs were long, like Grant's, his chest and upper body thick and muscular, like the men in Pauline's family. Between the two families, David had combined the best.

"About now, you'd be asking me how I'm enjoying school," David said. He smiled, an easy, wide smile. "And I'd say, oh, OK. Right?"

Grant watched his son and listened.

"Then you'd say, 'That's it? Just OK? I'm chipping in thousands of dollars for your education and that's the best you can do? OK?'"

The boy looked Grant in the face. "Actually, it's more than OK. I'm getting good grades. Now you would say 'Good grades aren't enough, that's not what a college education is all about. It's about learning. Are you learning, David? Are you getting an education?' Right dad?" David nodded at his father. "Well, yeah, I'm getting an education. I'm learning about history. Economics. I'm figuring out what I want to be, probably not what you'd hoped or planned for. I like the social sciences. I like being around people. I'm thinking I might go into some kind of social work."

Grant nodded. He smiled at his son.

"So that's OK with you then?" David said. "Social work?"

Grant nodded.

"Y'know, it's weird, talking to you and I'm doing all the talking. You used to do most of it, remember? You'd accuse me of not listening. But I was, dad. You just didn't see me or hear me listening. I wish I knew what you were thinking now, what you might say. You'd probably have something to say about social work, like I'd better learn to get by on a small salary. But you also used to tell me it's important that I do what interests me, what I like. You said life was too short to get up every day and dread going to work. You never dreaded going to work, did you dad?"

Grant shook his head.

"Listen, mom says this shrink you're seeing says you'll probably talk again. I hope so. Believe it or not, I do miss hearing your voice – I guess I even miss your lectures when I call home, though mom does a pretty good job filling in for you."

David grinned again. "You mind if I just sit here with you?"

Grant shook his head, smiled. He and his son sat on the porch together for a while, both of them listening to the family sounds inside the house, to Grant's wife, David's mother, gabbing with her own mother and father, the loud roar of laughter coming from William, likely in response to one of his own jokes.

"Mom's got a great family, y'know?" David said.

Grant nodded.

William pushed through the door. He held a can of beer and gazed out over the street, studying the neighborhood.

"Father and son talk?" he said, turning around and looking at Grant, then at David. He chuckled. William had inherited his own family's body style, opposite that of Pauline's family. William's family's bodies tapered generally from the waist down and from the waist up – large bellies, narrowing to the shoulders and to the feet. His face was round, his cheeks fat and red. His thick, blond hair curled over his ears. His smile, like the rest of him, was big.

"Mainly just a son talk," David said, grinning at his uncle.

"Oh, yeah," William said. He looked down at Grant, who glided slightly back and forth in the porch swing. "So, is silence so golden?"

He chuckled again, a low, throaty gurgle. "I'm joking," he said. "Seriously, we got a guy at work, a mute. Works in the mail room. Difference is, he's been mute all his life. It's probably harder having a voice and then losing it, huh?"

Grant watched William talk, watched his mouth move from beer can to forming words and back to the beer can. Foam clung to the hairs of his blonde moustache, which circled his mouth and joined up with a thick, curly beard. He was almost a blond Santa Claus.

"He's a good worker, though. A good guy. Great to get drunk with cuz he's such a good listener." William gurgled laughter again, took a long swig of his beer and then burped.

"I figure you don't have it so bad," William said to Grant. "You can have a night on the town and don't have to worry about any explanation the next morning. Me, I get the third degree just for takin' the trash out, she wonders what took me so long doin' it, what else did I do while I was out there, y'know?" William flashed a big, broad smile. "I love her though, don't get me wrong. But goddam it'd be nice to just come home and not have to say nothin', nothin' at all."

The big man opened the screen door, then turned around and said, "Least you never have to tell a lie." He winked, then went in and rejoined the family.

"He's a funny guy," David said. "I don't think he meant anything bad with what he just said. He's just being funny. He always made me laugh when I was a kid. Still does."

Grant nodded and smiled.

"I'm going to grab some pie while there's still some to grab. Food never stays long on the table with this family." David stood up. "You want anything?"

Grant shook his head and again had the front porch to himself. He stayed there, watching the clouds move above the peaked roofs of the houses up and down the sloping street, the occasional car drive down the middle of the road, between the cars parked on both sides, listening to the firecrackers pop as evening progressed. The sun moved westward, toward the ocean, toward evening, until the late-afternoon rays began to fill in the shady spots of the front porch, warming Grant's legs as he sipped on a can of beer and moved back and forth in the swing. Inside, the family conversation steadily, slowly, dwindled as the music of the stereo and the television continued to play.

Pauline stepped onto the porch. She sat down next to Grant on the swing. She patted him on the knee.

"You alright?" she said, her voice now a soft contrast to the booming house conversation earlier in the day.

Grant looked at her and nodded.

"I told you nobody would bother you," she said. "This family loves you, know that?"

Grant nodded.

"They're quite impressed about your gallery show. Especially Cliff and my mother. I really do think he's going to try and visit. That would be nice. You and Cliff always got along."

Grant and Pauline's entire family had always gotten along, but especially Cliff, whose interests leaned toward the intellectual. Grant and Cliff used to sit together on the porch, as the rest of the family reminisced and gossiped, discussing the political trends of the nation since they'd last been together – they shared a point of view that leaned Democratic but that was skeptical of the party in power at any particular time and of the big-money and corporate interests.

Grant would miss that discussion this year.

"I've been watching you out here," Pauline said. "It's interesting to watch you interact with different family members. With David, you were intent, it was almost as though you were talking to him. I could read your face. Without knowing what he was saying, I could almost hear you answer, you telling him to work hard in class, to take school seriously – just like you used to tell him. With my mother, I could see you listening, barely paying attention, being polite. With my father, your face was more alive, more expressive; you always used to ask him questions about his life. It's almost like, watching your face, I can see you sizing them up for a possible picture – a picture that would be more than a picture, like those ones we're going through at home now for your exhibit. A picture that almost talks to you. Then I saw you with William. I could tell from your face, you don't like him. With the others, I could tell you did like them, the way you answered them with your expression, with your eyes. You nodded or shook your head. You smiled. You frowned. You shrugged your shoulders. You've learned to communicate in different ways. You carried on a conversation – Grant, you can talk without speaking, when you want to. But with William, you said nothing. There was no expression. I guess that's deliberate, huh?"

Grant shrugged.

"I never noticed before," Pauline said. "Body language is an amazing thing, y'know?"

William came onto the porch, followed by Amy.

"I think we're going to walk up to the park and get a spot to watch the fireworks. You guys coming along?"

Grant looked at Pauline. His face said no.

"I think we'll watch them from here," Pauline said.

"You can't see them from here. We've

tried," William said.

Pauline looked at Grant again. He sighed. He stood up.

"Good," William said. "They put on a hell of a show. People bring their radios. The local PBS station plays the 1812 Overture, the one with the cannons, along with the fireworks."

William looked toward the door. "You folks coming?"

"We're coming," responded Pauline's mother. "Just wait. I want my cane, just in case."

Soon, the family emerged from the house, and all of them, led by William and Amy, then the parents, traipsed slowly up the incline of the hill to the top, then turned left, where they joined other walkers in the annual pilgrimage to the park and the Fourth of July fireworks display. Grant, Pauline and David brought up the rear, just behind Cliff and Sue. Vicki and Dom fell to the back; Grant and his son walked and listened as Pauline and Vicki yakked and laughed along the way, just as they had done as children.

XIV

It is always assumed by the empty-headed, who chatter about themselves for want of something better, that people who do not discuss their affairs openly must have something to hide.

– Honore de Balzac, Pere Goriot

Lindsay's column apparently had good readership. Or Andrew Bowman, director of the city's cultural arts program and of its East Side ArtScape Gallery, had a lot of friends. Or there were a lot of people in the city with no Friday night plans.

A mob moved through the gallery for the opening of Grant's photography exhibit, most of them faces Grant had never seen. But he recognized a few that emerged from the crowd to say hello to him or to grab a drink or scrap of food from the reception area, where Bowman had stationed Grant.

The exhibit room was a former storage area for a downtown warehouse. Bowman had covered the cement floors and pillars with wood and a stone facade resembling marble; he had hung track lighting from rows of parallel black bars that crisscrossed the room in a grid, but he'd left the high, wooden ceiling of the room exposed, like an open attic. The walls were all white. Grant's pictures hung in stark black frames, so the entire scene had a black-and-white art deco sort of look, all illuminated by chrome lighting fixtures.

A sign on an easel, black lettering on white posterboard, greeted the gallery visitors. It read: "ArtScape proudly presents 'City Faces,' photographs by Grant Baker." The name was apt; the exhibit was portraits done by Grant during his newspaper career – many of them recent.

One was the photo Grant had shot of the woman in the blue station wagon during that summer's wind storm. Boxed not only by the black edge of the gallery frame, the woman also was framed by the blue metal of the automobile. She peered into Grant's camera through the wet glass of the window, her gray hair swirling like the clouds barely mirrored in the glass of the window. Her cheeks were tinged with rouge that was a couple of shades lighter than the red of her lipstick. Wrinkles crossed her face like small cracks in parched earth. Her cheeks sunk in like desert crevices. But it was her eyes that were the focus of the photograph. Wide and alert, peering through her spectacles, they were moist, alive. They glistened, dark oases in an arid face, filled with panic as she hovered behind her window, afraid of the wailing storm beyond the glass, of the stranger who had stopped first to help her and then to photograph her, who stood just feet away from her now, aiming his camera at her like an alien hunter, an other-worldly gatherer of storm souls. Hers was an ancient face stripped of its dignity, of its pride, of its aged experience by its surrender to the terror of the storm and the camera-toting stranger.

A woman in blue jeans, leather sandals and a neatly buttoned and tucked white blouse gazed at the photograph, at the stark panic in the subject's face and eyes, at the serene title given the piece by Grant's wife: "Caught In A Summer Storm."

"This would make a good movie poster for that flick about tornadoes," the woman said to a man a few feet from her, lifting her glass of white wine to take a sip of the sparkling yellow liquid.

"Hey buddy." The voice was Ralston's. It came from Grant's left. The photographer looked up to see the reporter standing a few feet away, facing the food trays, piling cubes of yellow and white cheese, some carrot sticks, onto a small glass plate. "Looks like you got a hit on your hands."

Tracy was with Ralston. She was in her usual work garb – a pair of casual slacks, tennis shoes, blue shirt beneath a tan vest. She nodded at Grant, flashed him a quick grin, then turned and asked the man at the makeshift bar for a bottle of beer. Ralston also wore his work outfit – dark slacks, white shirt, polished lace shoes. The only thing missing was the tie – Derek Fisher insisted that all his reporters wear a tie on duty; photographers were exempt from the rule because of the harsher conditions they sometimes faced.

Creativity has its freedoms.

"All the hoi polloi are here," Ralston said, carrying his plate of food to Grant and Pauline – Grant in his suit and tie, Pauline in a dressy blue skirt and white blouse.

"Hi Mr. Ralston," Pauline said.

"Mrs. Baker. Nice show. Your husband does good work."

"Thanks." Pauline nodded at Ralston, who, with Tracy, stood next to Grant and Pauline for a few moments, observing the crowd gathered in the gallery. A general murmur filled the room, blending with the violin music that seeped out of speakers attached to the corners of the room and aimed at its center. Turtlenecks, pressed denim, khaki, fashionably wrinkled cotton, vests, ties, grubby jeans, sandals, heels, nose studs, ear hoops – Grant's audience, like his framed faces, was a cross section of the city's culture, a mixture of black and white and brown and yellow pigments moving from frame to frame, studying the pictures of humanity that inhabited their community, their world, their sphere of power and influence and artistic collaboration and competition. The room was like a disco but without the beat or the dancing – a mass of people with drinks in their hands observing each other along with the faces that hung on the wall.

Pauline had labeled the photo of the old immigrant farmer "Riverton Gardener."

The picture was of the elderly man Grant had snapped working in his garden. The sun shone on the old man's gray ponytail that hung over his dark neck from beneath a straw cowboy hat. His head was turned toward the camera, a cigarette poking from his lips, the smoke from its tip forming a straight thread of gray that seemed to connect the man's thin lips to the blue sky above him. Grant had cropped the photo tightly

THE SILENT TREATMENT

on the man's face so you could not see the hoe in his hands, the dry earth beneath his feet, the green shoots of vegetation he'd been working. His eyes were thin slits in brown skin that was crinkled and taut over an oval skull. They were eyes that were leery and questioning – distrustful of this photographer who had stumbled into the village on a quiet summer day, poking here and there with his camera, disrupting the life of people who had established their own community, their own lives, away and separate from that of the city – simple lives of work, families, churches, of Spanish and tortillas and home-grown vegetables, of pride in their separation from the rest of the community. They were eyes that warned the stranger not to tread or probe too deeply into this world, not to question its ways or expose its values and secrets, eyes that guarded a different culture, that barely concealed the distrust and hatred that existed in the shadows, in the back yards, behind the closed doors and walls of the village.

"Old dude's been baked by the sun," said a man in a black shirt held closed by silver buttons beneath a brown sport coat. He wore a full beard trimmed close to the skin; his eyes studied the photograph through the thin lenses of silver-framed glasses. "Looks like he's had his share of tequilas in his life, look at that nose." The man chuckled to his companion, a woman who wore a matching black blouse with pearl buttons and a satiny white jacket.

"Hey, y'know who he looks like?" the woman said. "Your cousin Raymond. Yeah. Look at it. That's Raymond, a Mexican Raymond."

"OK," Walt said to Grant as he approached the reception area. "Where'd you hide the whiskey? I come to your goddam picture show, I don't want this white wine and cheese crap. I want a shot of whiskey and a pickled egg."

Grant's boss grinned through his thick moustache and stuck out his hand to be shaken. "Hello Pauline," he said. "Good to see you."

"Walt," she replied. "Nice to see a familiar face. I never saw so many people in one place that I didn't know."

"And that you don't need to bother to know, believe me," Walt said, opening a bottle of beer. He took a couple of long gulps; bits of white foam stuck to his moustache. "These sorts of things bring out all the phonies. No offense, Grant. I don't suppose I can smoke in here. I didn't think so." Walt grinned and took another couple of drinks of his beer.

Grant nodded at his fellow photographer, then spotted a familiar blonde head among the crowd. Lindsay was standing in front of one of the pictures – a photograph of her own face staring out at the crowd, an extreme closeup of her eyes, shot at the time that she was sitting naked in her living room with Grant's camera lens probing her eyes. She glanced at Grant, their gaze met; she eyed him for a moment, then turned her face back to her portrait, to the clean lines of her nose, the perfect complexion, the blue eyes that had looked into Grant's head, inside his skin, that evening in her apartment. Grant watched her as she moved to the next portrait, and then the next, studying each.

She stopped in front of a picture Grant had taken nearly a decade ago, of a prisoner who sat on the far side of a wooden table in a prison interview room as a reporter talked to the prisoner about his impending execution on death row. Grant had used a zoom lens to focus on the prisoner's face; the walls behind the man were a blurry, smudged white; his face was dark in the dim lighting of the room. His whiskers were a shadow on his lean face. His teeth were yellow, except for the black space in front where he'd lost one in a run-in with a fellow inmate. His narrow, dark eyes were dull, lifeless, hopeless. The picture's title was "Death Row," arrived at by Pauline after consultation with Walt, who had spent a couple of weeks helping Pauline and Grant put the exhibit together, who had helped provide background information for many of the portraits in the exhibit.

Lindsay, notebook in hand, moved from photo to photo, stopping to study each one: a 10-year-old girl with the face of an old woman, in remission from leukemia but who would be dead within the year – her brown, sparkling eyes the one sign of hope and life in a pale face of despair and resignation; a welfare mother, her cheeks fat beneath slits of eyes filled with a web of bloody veins, her nose wide and pocked, her chin folded in pleats of fat; a homeless street man, his eyes sunken in dark shadows, the furrows in his face tracing the events of his life: perhaps war duty in Vietnam, perhaps a bout with cancer, perhaps a daughter who had died. Pictures don't talk, they just suggest.

A middle-aged man and woman stared at the photo of the welfare mother.

"That's such a sad picture," the woman, her brown, straight hair speckled with gray, said to the man.

"Yeah," the man said back. "It's sad alright, that I got a job and she don't and my taxes pay her rent. Can we get outa here?"

Lindsay wrote notes as she strolled among the photographs; she never looked toward Grant, whose eyes followed her route along the walls and frames of his work, of the 30 or so photographs of faces that Grant had documented in his career as a newspaper photographer and portraitist.

The final portion of the exhibit was a set of four photographs. One, titled "The Graduate," was a picture Grant had shot of a high school senior, a girl who told Grant she planned to study veterinary medicine in college; she wanted to devote her practice to working with animal shelters, with disowned pets, with animals who had no owners and little chance. Her face, framed by shining brown hair that draped down to her shoulders, was bright, eager; her eyes looked into a future of success. Her complexion was unmarred, the outline of her face clear and certain; the focus on her blue eyes as she gazed into the camera was one of certainty and clarity. Next to her was a photograph, titled "Premature Death." This picture depicted a severed head of a girl, her yellow hair matted in blood and dirt, her nose sliced open with white, blood-stained cartilage protruding from the nasal cavity. Her mouth was a black, open abyss; blood spattered the corners of her lips, which were spread apart like the mouth of a hooked fish. Her eyeballs had sprung from their sockets, which were dark, bloody pools; her face was a mass of blood and bruises, with a couple of clear spots of flesh standing out like tiny pink islands in a swirl of guts. The bottom of the neck was a gash of blood and skin, with white gristle poking out. Below and to the left of these two photographs was a close-up of Edvard Munch's painting "The Scream." In this picture, Grant had cropped out the background and had zoomed in on the head, the upside-down teardrop figure of the yellow-green face of the portrait's subject, a ghostlike figure clutching the side of its face with open, fingerless hands, its mouth gaping wide in an oval, silent scream, its eyes wide pits with tiny black specks in them, all set in a swirl of confusion and light, pastel colors – the figure resembled an alien with its clean, undefined lines, its other-worldly curves and arcs. The final picture in the set, titled "Self Portrait," was of Grant, an unsmiling mouth, its lips sealed in direct contrast to the open, screaming mouth of the figure in the neighboring photograph, the face covered with a gray-brown, two-day growth of stubble, again in contrast to the clean, bald figure of Munch's

painting. The eyes, also opposites of the screamer, were narrow and thin, offering but a glimpse
of whatever lay behind them.

Lindsay held her notebook to her side as
she studied the four pictures, her eyes moving
from one to another and then back, her head
slowly shaking back and forth, until finally she
spun around, glanced through the crowd briefly,
then headed for the exit, where Grant saw her
blonde head disappear into the night.

"Very nice set of pictures, Mr. Baker," said
a voice to Grant's right. He turned his head, saw
a woman in a red blouse and tan slacks standing
there, a glass of wine in her hand. He gazed at her
as she smiled at him. Then she turned and was
gone, part of the general crowd again.

Later, as the bar and wait crew gathered
the drink glasses, plates, napkins and cleaned up
the place, Grant and Pauline stood in the middle
of the room, surrounded by the faces hanging on
the wall. Bowman was at the back of the room,
laughing between comments into the small, portable telephone.

Pauline sighed. "It looks like you have
what you always wanted," she said to her husband. She smiled at him.

Grant let his eyes roam among the photographs, his mind still seeing the crowded room, hearing the buzz of the conversation about his work, about him – the gasps when people reached the final four pictures of the exhibit.

"A few people asked me about the meaning of that ghastly head and the painting of the screaming man," Pauline said. "I didn't know what to tell them, Grant. I assume there's a meaning there, but it's beyond me."

Bowman's footsteps clopped across the floor as he chatted into his telephone. Grant put his arm through Pauline's and tugged her toward the exit.

"I suppose we're going to meet Walt at that bar," Pauline said.

Grant nodded.

"You know, I quit going to those bars with you a long time ago," she said. "But I'll go this time. This is your night, Grant. This is what you've been working for. God knows you've earned it."

Outside the gallery door, they looked back in, saw Bowman still yakking on his cell phone, saw the myriad of portraits, a gathering of faces, hung on the wall. Then Bowman marched to a rear wall, flipped a switch, and Grant's exhibit vanished into blackness.

Pauline and Grant drove in silence to the

272   THE SILENT TREATMENT

Club Cafe. Traffic lined the downtown streets, radios blaring, car windows down, folks shouting and laughing, filling the city with noise that bounced among the dark, closed buildings of the business district. They drove by the office tower where Grant had photographed raindrops, where he had focused and clicked his shutter on a minute bead of water that contained the universe, where the security guard, suspecting Grant of terrorism or business espionage or of trespassing, had smashed Grant's camera and knocked the photographer cold. They turned off and headed for the old warehouse district, found a parking spot in front of the Club Cafe just as a car was pulling out.

The inside of the bar was packed. Grant recognized some of the folks who had been at the gallery – a black dress with a neckline that made a deep vee from the neck, splitting the breasts and coming to a point just above the stomach; a pair of blue jeans and white shirt filled with silver buckles and chains and ending in a set of brown leather cowboy boots; a see-through white blouse behind which posed a pair of small breasts and a pewter medallion. A path cleared as Grant and Pauline walked through the bar. They spotted Walt, Ralston and Tracy at a booth; Ralston stood up and waved to them.

Grant and Pauline slid into the wooden seat across from Grant's three coworkers.

"Very nice show, pal," Ralston said.

Walt nodded in agreement. "You showed 'em," he said. "Art ain't just paint on canvas." He winked at Grant.

Tracy added a nod and a grin. "Goddam if I ever let this old bastard take an assignment away from me again," she said, nudging Walt in the side with her elbow. "Seriously, Grant, it was a fine show. Except, I'm curious."

Grant looked at Tracy.

"I don't understand the bloody head," Tracy said. "I know, you'd probably tell me the interpretation is mine to make. But I still don't get it. Wasn't that the girl who got hit in that accident a while back?"

"The one and the same," Walt said. "I don't understand it either, didn't when I was helping Grant and Pauline put the show together. But you gotta admit, it's one dramatic photo."

"That it is," Tracy said, lifting her beer bottle for a toast as the waiter brought a tray of drinks to the booth.

"Another round please," Ralston told the waiter. "We got something else to celebrate tonight."

"Oh?" Walt said. "And what's that? Has the paper been sold to a human being?"

Ralston grinned.

"So tell 'em," Tracy said. "Tell 'em."

"I finished my book," Ralston said. He looked at each of them, a wide grin on his face.

Nobody said anything.

"Sat up all night last night polishing it. It's ready."

"Great," Walt said. "Two artists in our midst. Congratulations, Ralston. And what's the baby's name?"

"Uh uh." Ralson shook his head. "That's all you get out of me. You know I don't talk about my novel writing, Walt. I'll tell you this much. It's called 'The Shakespeare Murders.' " He grinned. "It's got some great double entendres in it, you know, and ironies. Like the notes the killer leaves for the cops – 'Here's my latest pound of flesh' is one he leaves on a corpse discovered by – get this, the main cop's name is Sam Johnson. Great, huh? That's all you guys'll get out of me, though."

Grant raised his glass of beer toward the reporter, who lifted his bottle and clicked it to Grant's glass, then to Pauline's, Walt's and Tracy's.

The waiter brought the next round and the five of them got to work on their drinks – beers for Grant, Ralston and Tracy, a martini for Walt and ginger ale for Pauline.

Somebody yelled for Ralston from the far end of the bar. Ralston looked up, saw the face that had yelled. He grabbed Tracy and pulled her out of the booth with him. "There's Angelo," he said. "C'mon. Let's tell him the news."

That left Walt facing Grant and Pauline.

"I think the kid's not much longer for the newspaper," he said. "I guess he's got some talent. I mean, he's a good reporter. But geez, a goddam novelist."

"What kind of novel is it?" Pauline said.

"Who knows? I think it's a mystery. I asked him once, he said talking about his writing robbed it of something. Sort of like the Indians used to believe that taking their picture robbed their souls. Something like that. Listen, folks, I'm an old man. I'm tired."

Pauline smiled. "You and me both," she said. "It's been a long time since I've come out to a bar. You know what, though? This kind of place, it's always the same. The same people, the same noise, the same drunks."

"The same assholes," Walt said, grinning.

"All of the guys hitting on the women – or on other guys, these days. The wannabes and the has beens all under one roof, all getting drunk, all celebrating their futures or forgetting their pasts."

"My," Pauline said. "We have a philosopher among us, Grant." She looked at her husband. "I have to use the ladies' room. Do you mind if we leave after that?"

Grant nodded.

Walt stood up with Pauline. "I'm outa here," he said. He yawned.

"Thanks for your help with this," Pauline said.

"Hey, I enjoyed it. I'm glad to see Grant showing his stuff. He deserves it." He looked at the photographer, who had remained seated in the booth. "You do, buddy. See you at work Monday."

Grant nodded and smiled at Walt. He and Pauline watched the Bulletin's photo chief walk out of the bar. Pauline looked down at Grant. "I'll be right back," she said.

Grant watched his wife walk through the crowd and into it, then watched her head, all he could see of her now, as she went to the restrooms at the back of the bar. He listened to the noise of the place, the drinkers shouting to each other, the laughter, the speakers pushing an electric blues guitar, a harmonica, a deep bass, through the crowd. He took a long drink of his beer and closed his eyes. Many of these people had been his tonight, had looked at his work, discussed it, debated it. Forever in his mind now he had a snapshot of a crowd, a gathering of faces, all of them there for him.

"Congratulations."

Grant recognized the voice, looked up and saw Lindsay's face.

"Quite a show," she said. "Though I have some issues with it. Your use of my face in it, for one – without my permission, I might add. No model's release, right?"

Grant scooted over in the booth, as though to make room for Lindsay.

"No, I won't be joining you and your wife," Lindsay said. She eyed Grant up and down. "Really, I just came over to tell you one thing, Grant. No man has ever walked out on me the way you did that night. Never."

Lindsay lifted her glass of red wine, took a drink and slowly licked its residue from her lips. Then she held the wine glass over Grant's head, tipped it and poured it onto him. She set the glass on the table, turned and walked away.

Grant heard the gasps, the laughter, felt the eyes of the place on him for a few moments, the wine dripping down his face. Then he looked toward the back end of the bar and saw Pauline staring at him, her mouth open and round like the silent screamer in Munch's painting, then slowly closing. She came across the room to him as the noise came back to the room. He heard Lindsay's voice somewhere, near the bar, ordering a fresh drink as she seemed to have misplaced hers – more laughter, snorting, sneering laughter.

"That was that art critic wasn't it?" Pauline said. She remained standing at the edge of the booth.

Grant stared down into his glass of beer. He picked it up and drank down the rest of it. He stood up, took Pauline by the elbow and gently pulled her toward the door.

"Why'd she do that, Grant?"

The two of them went outside. The air was cool, filled with the buzzing of the bar, the glow of the city lights. They walked to the car a few feet away. Grant opened the passenger door for Pauline, then went around and slid in behind the wheel. They rolled their windows down and stared at the outside of the bar, at its window front where a group of men and women stood talking, holding their drinks. They saw Ralston's body, and Tracy's next to his; Ralston was talking to the group, Tracy stood next to him, watching him, adoring him.

"You sleep with that woman?" Pauline said.

Grant looked at her.

"You're not answering me, Grant."

Her husband shook his head.

"Hell. You couldn't have insulted her, not when you can't talk. So I guess I'll never know why she just poured wine on your head," Pauline said, "except that it had nothing to do with sex. I'm glad of that much."

Grant's wife sighed as he started the engine.

"I don't know if I can take this kind of lifestyle Grant. I mean, we've been there, remember? The bars, the drunks, the hangers-on. I like things the way they are, or were, Grant."

Pauline reached her hand across the seat and laid it on Grant's leg as he put the car into gear and drove back through the city toward home.

XV

Secret truth is by silence revealed.

– John Dryden

Walt was sitting at his desk, scanning negatives into the computer, when Grant walked in.

"Hey buddy," the chief photographer said. "Am I glad to see you. Budget meeting's in a couple hours, and so far I ain't got squat. I need a good feature shot. Maybe you can find something going on at the park, you know, kids playin' or something. I'm hurtin', Grant. Before you go, you got a love letter there." Walt motioned to the latest copy of the Metro sitting on his desk.

Grant leafed through the newspaper until he arrived at an inside back page carrying the headline, "For Art's Sake."

This time, he was the lead item in Lindsay's column.

"From time to time," her column began, "we make a mistake in judgment, an error in our perception, and we find it necessary to erase a goof. An artist will paint over a canvas and begin again, a ceramicist will destroy a bowl and restart with fresh clay – this columnist needs to eradicate previous comments made in this space about photographer Grant Baker.

"The man's a fraud upon the art world," Lindsay's column continued. "Following his showing of photos at the Bulletin's lobby that accompanied B. Sinclair Ralston's series on immigrant children – photos that this column praised – Baker has opened an exhibit of photographs at the city's ArtScape Gallery in the East Side cultural district that is an amateurish gathering of portraits that offer perhaps a picture or two worthy of study, but little more."

"What'd you do to that broad?" Walt said, coming around from behind his desk to read over Grant's shoulder. "Last I knew you were best of chums."

Grant kept reading.

"The exhibit, for the most part, is portraits of victims – victims of our economic system, of nature, of fellow human beings. For his focus on this kind of subject, the photographer is to be commended. But my applause stops there.

"The most puzzling aspect of this exhibit is the final frames, a quartet of photos that apparently are supposed to make a point of some kind – but if there is an artistic statement in this gaudy display, it is elusive. The four photos include a self portrait of the photographer, a picture of a soon-to-be high school graduate, a rip-off from the world of painting in which Baker has photographed Edvard Munch's 'The Scream' with a tight focus on the artist's screaming head, and a gory photograph of a decapitated head – the head, I am told, of a teenage girl who was killed in a fatal automobile accident just this spring.

"Obviously, the artist – and calling Baker an artist is doing him a great justice in this case – is trying to tell us something. We can't ask him, as he is physically incapable of speech; so we have to let his so-called work speak for itself.

"What it says to me is little more than shock value. Perhaps it is a scream for help from the artist – we'll leave that speculation to the psychiatrists – or perhaps it is the photographic equivalent of radio shock-jock disc jockeys. I don't know, but we'll leave this exhibit with this observation: No words can do justice to this travesty. The biggest favor we can do for this exhibit is to give it our silence."

"Wow," Walt said. "Welcome to the fickle world of art, buddy."

Grant closed the newspaper and stuffed it into his camera bag. He stood up and headed for the door.

"Be back in a couple hours buddy," Walt said.

Grant went out of the photo lab and into the newsroom, then headed for the exit.

"Grant." Walt's voice stopped Grant. He turned around.

Walt came closer to the photographer, stopping a couple of feet from him.

"You OK?"

Grant stood inside the door, motionless, his eyes on Walt.

"Listen. She's just a crazy broad. Don't let this get to you. I saw the same exhibit she did, and I thought it kicked ass. And so did some of the folks I heard talking about it at the gallery, and at the bar later. She's got some kind of bug up her ass, that's all. Ignore it."

Grant turned and went through the door and out onto the parking lot, off to find children playing, lovers walking, dogs romping – something cute and colorful for the front page of the next morning's Bulletin – and then on to his afternoon session with Dr. Clevenger.

A couple of hours later, the psychiatrist

had a puzzled look on his face as Grant sat opposite him that afternoon. The doctor clasped his hands over his mouth, covering his chin, his neck, his Adam's apple, and he studied Grant as though for the first time.

"I think you have some issues," the psychiatrist said. "In fact, I know you do – know for the first time now, Grant."

The doctor took a deep breath and slowly exhaled it through the filter of the fists in front of his mouth. Then he lowered his hands, laid them flat, palms down, on his desk.

"I stopped in to see your exhibit at that gallery," Clevenger said. "You're a first-rate photographer, Grant. First rate. Each of those portraits told a story – much of it a downer, I'm afraid. I saw a lot of desperation, poverty, despair in your work. It had its bright spots, for sure – but I don't know that I've ever seen such intensity in a photograph, Grant, such a depth of feeling and emotion."

Grant watched the psychiatrist as he talked, studied his face, saw an impassive man, like jurors he had studied, who observe and listen to testimony, take it in, consider it. The doctor, maybe for the first time, was watching Grant as though listening to him, hearing him – though

Grant remained expressionless.

"That last sequence was something again, Grant," the doctor said, his Adam's apple moving slightly now as he took a swallow. He looked into Grant's face as he continued talking. "That set of pictures was produced by a troubled mind. Grant, is there any possibility, any chance, you can try to write something down for me?"

Grant showed no response.

"A nod, then?"

Nothing.

"C'mon, Grant. You used to at least nod for me. In fact, we were making good progress, I thought. Your face was becoming more expressive visit by visit. You could smile, frown, shrug. Why, we practically had conversations, Grant. Now, will you give me a nod?"

Grant stared back at the psychiatrist.

"Listen, Grant, those pictures are troubling. That bloody head. What was that about? The painting of the guy screaming. Then the beautiful young woman, the high school senior. And you. What is your role in all of this, in this sequence?"

The doctor shook his head back and forth, slowly. He clasped and unclasped his hands. He picked up his pen, tapped the end of it on the desk.

"Grant, do those pictures have anything to do with something that happened, something that took away your ability to speak, your desire to communicate? I've concluded, Grant, that part of this problem of yours is a desire on your part – you've not only lost the ability to speak, but you've withdrawn from the world. And damn it if those pictures aren't the clue as to why. They're like a jigsaw puzzle of your brain, Grant, a smooth-sided, four-piece, rectangular picture that, pieced together, will tell me what the hell's going on inside of you."

The doctor leaned back in his chair, gazed up at the ceiling so that his Adam's apple jutted from his neck. It poked into the air, like a smooth, round rock, as the doctor looked at the ceiling and pondered.

Finally: "I don't know, Grant. I don't know what to do. Your first visit here, your wife suggested hypnosis. Maybe that would help. Maybe I should refer you to a man I know who works with hypnosis. How would you feel about that?"

Grant gazed at the doctor, listening to him, studying his face as though sizing it up for a portrait – a picture of a puzzled, confused man, his eyes filled with questions.

"The thing is, I feel like you're close to breaking out of this thing. I have seen progress – I think this photo exhibit is progress, I think it is you trying to communicate with us. I'm dead sure of it – so why the sudden silence, Grant?"

The doctor smiled. "You know what I mean. I've never known you to be anything other than silent. I mean, now you're gone totally incommunicado. Period. Blank. Why?"

Clevenger sighed, glanced at his watch. "Our time's about up, Grant. I'm going to plan on seeing you again. I'm going to talk to your wife, maybe suggest we try the hypnosis route. I'm going to consult with some people, see if they have any ideas. This would almost be considered severe, if you weren't doing everything else that you are – staging photo exhibits, excelling at your job, doing fine with Pauline. You're a riddle, Mr. Baker."

Then Clevenger sat still for a few moments, just watching Grant. Grant watched back. The psychiatrist smiled.

"You'll be glad to know, I'm playing the piano again," Clevenger said. "I don't mean an occasional midnight rhapsody. I mean, I've been going home and practicing nights. Really practicing. I've bought some sheet music; I've been working on improvisations."

Grant listened passively, politely, to the doctor talk about his music.

"I think I'm playing with more passion, more feeling, than I ever have," Clevenger said. "I don't know why. But man, when I go into a blues riff, I can feel it. The music is coming from way down inside of me now. It used to just come out of my head; I'd follow the notes, the timing, count out my rests and do everything technically well. But now, I might linger over a note a half-beat longer, just because I like the way it feels. I don't know, it's hard to explain. But the piano suddenly, it's like the keys have some kind of life – maybe you know what I mean, maybe when you pick up your camera and you see something in a way you haven't seen it before, and your camera becomes a part of you, of the inside of you. I think you do understand, Grant. I think you understand every word I say; I think you feel every picture you take – and I think I understand better now, because of my piano. Does that make sense? Nod, Grant. Tell me if it makes sense or not."

Grant didn't move. The only sound in the room was the steady tick-ticking of the grandfather clock.

"Alright, Grant," Clevenger said, followed

by a sigh. "I find it interesting, though, that my attitude toward my piano playing coincides with the time I've been seeing you. Stop at the desk outside and get your appointment card. I'll see you next time."

Grant stood up. He looked down at the doctor, framed him in his mind's eye, posed him, a picture of a man in a dress shirt and tie, a thin, pale face, his hands folded on his desk, looking up into the lens with eyes full of doubt. Grant turned and walked through the door, closing it behind him with a gentle click like the snapping of an electronic shutter.

XVI

Silence is the mother of everything that has come from the Depth. And Silence kept quiet about what she was unable to describe: the Unspeakable.

– Clement of Alexandria

Pauline heard the clear timbre of a vibra-phone coming from the study as she entered the kitchen after her faculty meeting. She could feel Grant in there, in his chair, listening to the music. She put her purse on the kitchen table and walked into the darkness of the study, saw Grant sitting there.

"Hello," she said. "You hungry?"

Grant sat motionless. She went into the study and stood in front of him.

"Don't I get a smile?" his wife said.

Grant looked into her face with an empty expression on his.

Pauline sighed. "OK," she said. "What is it tonight, why the silent treatment? Something go wrong at work?"

No reply in Grant's face.

"Something I said, didn't say, something I did, didn't do? C'mon, Grant, even without your voice I can tell now when you're in one of your moods. And you're in one. What is it?"

She sat down in her chair next to Grant's. "Dr. Clevenger called me today. He told me you seem to have regressed. That was his word. I can see now, though, it's just you being you. In one of your moods, I guess, which'll pass."

She stood up, went into the kitchen and saw the Metro sitting on the table. It was open to Lindsay's column. Pauline pulled out a chair, sat down and read the piece as Grant listened to the Modern Jazz Quartet album on the city's jazz radio station. Milt Jackson's vibes rang through the room. After a while, she returned to the study and sat down again. She peered out the window, its curtains drawn. The air beyond the front porch was dark; it was late evening.

"This woman has some kind of problem," Pauline said. "She's not very nice."

Vibe and piano chords hung in the darkness.

"Surely you're not taking this stuff to heart. Grant, you know that's a good display. You know it. Walt said so. He's never lied to you, has he? Hasn't he told you when your photographs don't work?"

Grant sat motionless, listening to his wife.

Pauline got up from her chair. She stood in front of Grant, looked down at him, listening with him to the soft brushes on the snare drum, the bass that growled beneath John Lewis' piano work and Jackson's gentle mallets. She reached down and took Grant's hand, squeezed it in hers.

"Doctor Clevenger asked me if I want to try a hypnosis session. I didn't know. Then he said maybe it was time to send you to some kind of specialist." She gave his hand another squeeze.

"You want to try and see someone else?"

Grant did not respond.

"I don't know, Grant. Things aren't so bad. If you think about it, good things started happening to you after you lost your voice. Work started going better; you're mainly shooting news and features now. You had that wonderful series with B. Sinclair. You've got your own show in an exhibit – and I don't care what that Lindsay person says. It's a good show. I heard a lot of good comments about it. People don't understand that bloody head, and neither do I. The doctor thinks it and that scream painting mean something. Maybe we should try someone else?"

Grant looked up at his wife's face in the

dark of the room. Simmering jazz chords surrounded them like water; they stared at each other in a dark pool of music.

"I think maybe everything that's happened has a purpose. I know you don't believe that, Grant. But I do. I can't believe we're here for nothing. Listen to that music. You used to tell me you like the improvisation, the spontaneity of jazz, that it gave the musician a chance to explore. But listen to it, Grant. It also has structure. It has a key that the musicians follow. It's going somewhere; the song was written down onto paper and given form, a plan, then the musicians give it life and meaning through their interpretation, their direction. That's what we're doing with our lives. I know you don't believe this, but we have a purpose, there's something intended for our existence, and then we sort of improvise on that. But it's all part of a plan. I think all of this might be a plan for you, Grant. You've got your job, plus now you've got your show. Don't pay any attention to what that woman wrote about you, about your work. You know what you're doing – and now, you're there. It's all there for you, Grant."

Pauline squeezed her husband's hand one more time, then placed it on his knee. She went back to the kitchen. The kitchen light streamed into the dining room, throwing long furniture shadows across the floor. Grant closed his eyes and listened to the music. Pauline turned off the kitchen light.

"I'm going upstairs to read in bed for awhile. Why don't you c'mon up?"

Grant felt her dark form move through the living room, listened to her footsteps pad up the carpeted stairway and then creak through the hallway to the bedroom.

He sat in his chair, listened to the jazz quartet in the darkness, to the crisp applause that followed the tune. Grant closed his eyes and let the music cover him like a soothing blanket. There was silence for a few moments as the Modern Jazz Quartet session ended and the disc jockey moved to a Wes Montgomery set. The jazz musician strummed some guitar chords that rang familiarly in Grant's mind. The octave pattern of the chords struck a memory in the darkness, in the recesses of Grant's silence.

The guitar notes, flowing smoothly in the night shadows of Grant's living room, took Grant to a two-lane rural road. He drove in the cool air of the countryside, a breeze blowing across the front seat from open window to open window, carrying the scent of plowed dirt, spring perfume. A Wes Montgomery blues played on the car's CD player, the jazzy riffs skimming along the road as Grant drove through the flat farmland, the barns and fences and silos passing his window as though motoring through color photographs of rural America, each farm a still-life image.

The woman – girl really, she was just a senior in high school – had lain naked on the patch of grass in front of the oak tree, the wild flowers behind and to the left of her, staring into his camera. He focused on the yellow and blue butterfly tattoo at the top of her left breast. The image of her flesh, the curved horizon of her neck, shoulders and legs, teased him still as he sped down the meandering asphalt, through the fields of young alfalfa, soy beans, corn. His mind flipped through her poses, focused on the smooth, young skin of her body, the lush, dark valley between her thighs. He had spent most of the session shooting her standing among the wildflowers, leaning in a pose against the tree trunk; she had chosen the spot for the shoot, had met him there in the morning; she wanted a country setting for her senior picture. Then, when Grant thought they'd finished, she asked him to take a few more shots, just for her.

"I have some money," she said. "I'll pay for this set myself. I want it for my boyfriend. He's overseas right now, in the Army."

Grant listened as she explained her request for the nude picture session.

"We're going to get married when he comes home. My parents want me to wait, go to college. But we've already decided. He gave me a ring." She reached into her pocket, took out the small diamond ring and pushed it onto her finger. "I want you to take my picture for him, and I want to wear the ring for him. Nothing but the ring. Will you do it?"

Grant looked at her, at her youth, her clean complexion, her fresh brown hair, the beauty spot below her right eye, the dimples at each end of her lips like parentheses.

"Here." She reached into her purse, took out her wallet. She handed her driver's license to Grant. "I'm old enough. Look at the birth date."

Grant agreed to take the pictures. The girl undressed, casually, unashamedly, carefully piling her clothes out of the way, as Grant put a fresh roll of film into his camera and set it up on the tripod. She stood next to the tree naked, as she had posed minutes before in her dress for her high school yearbook portrait. She smiled into the camera, a long-distance smile, an I-love-you smile, for her enlisted boyfriend. She lay on the grass, her hip jutting into the air like a rolling hill on the horizon, her breasts firm and full and young, the yellow and blue butterfly just on top of the grass like the real thing sitting there in the breeze. Grant shot several photos of the naked girl.

"He's going to love these," she said as she dressed. "It'll help him stop from being lonely at night." She smiled at Grant, an innocent high-school grin tinged with the mature woman she had become, the adult she would be, officially, in another few months when she left high school and began her life adventure.

Grant drove the country road, blues guitar notes streaming through his car with the wind, as he stared into the sky and pavement ahead. He saw the girl's breasts, gawked at the memory of her wonderful naked breasts with the butter-fly, when he heard the horn blaring at him, saw the black sedan coming at him, its headlights a couple of sudden panicked eyes, its grill a grimac-ing mouth, saw his own car on the wrong side of the road heading straight for the sedan. He jerked the steering wheel, pulling his car back to the right side of the road, just as the black sedan screeched, went off the road and flashed by. He heard a high-pitched scream that punctured the air, then the loud whump, followed by the crash of metal, the tinkling of glass. He hit his own brakes, pulled off the road and turned to look at the scene.

The sedan was a smashed, warped pile of black metal and bent chrome. He automatically grabbed his camera bag and pushed open his door, leaving the engine running. He walked quickly across the road. He looked up and down the pavement, saw empty lanes in both directions as the black road faded into the distant green and brown horizon. The front of the car was wrapped around the tree; the metal was bare, the paint scraped away, where the vehicle had come up against the bark. The entire front of the car was rippled like an accordion. Grant rushed to the driver's side of the car. He saw a pair of legs in blood-soaked blue jeans. He saw an arm. He smelled the blood, the simmering engine, burnt rubber, hot oil. He jerked on the front door; it wouldn't give. He pulled again, yanked as hard as he could; with a squawk, the door broke free and flew open. Shards of glass flew through the air. A head, blonde and fleshy, red with blood, rolled out the door and plopped to the ground at Grant's feet, its bloody eye sockets peering at him.

Grant's mouth opened. He turned his head to the sky, his mouth open wide, struggling to scream. But nothing came out. The only sound was Wes Montgomery's guitar making octave chords in the still, warm air, as Grant stood there, his mouth open, empty. He looked at the death scene, picked up his camera and did what came naturally to him, working the controls of the camera. He walked around the car, pointing the lens, focusing; he clicked, clicked, clicked the shutter, until he heard the banshee police siren in the distance.

Now Grant's mouth was screaming silence into the dark night of his study. He sat up straight in the chair, gasping, sobbing, searching for his voice to yell out to the sky about the dead girl, about the awful stench, the bloody flesh and bone and meat that had been a human being. The red light of the stereo system shone in the darkness. The guitar played on the stereo, mingling with the notes, like the notes that surrounded him that morning, the electric chords that hung in the air as Grant stood next to the smashed car, the dead girl, in the sunlight.

Grant felt arms, Pauline's arms, around him.

"What is it Grant?" Her voice was loud, shaking. "Grant, Grant. I heard you sobbing upstairs. What is it?"

Grant, his mouth still open, stared at his wife. Tears rolled down his face.

"You're crying, Grant. I heard you, heard you upstairs. This is wonderful. It's wonderful. You're crying. I heard you, Grant. I felt you scream."

Pauline pulled Grant to the floor, sat down facing him, pulled him to her; she took his head to her chest and caressed his hair. As the picture of the dead girl, blood bubbling from the red and white guts of her neck, lingered – he could hear Pauline's heart beat. As he saw himself shooting photographs, instinctively walking around and around the perimeter of the accident clicking his shutter open and shut, recording the death scene, his head reeling, bending over to throw up a few feet from the severed head as the cops pulled up – he could feel Pauline's pulse, her warm body, her arms holding him tightly. As he heard again the approaching sirens bringing emergency personnel whose questions he could not answer, who informed police officers that he appeared to be in shock – Pauline's voice resonated from within her chest.

"Oh my God, you were crying. It's wonderful, Grant."

Pauline pulled back, stared into Grant's face.

"Do you understand, Grant?"

Grant nodded.

"Talk to me Grant. Tell me about your nightmare. Was it a nightmare? Grant. It wasn't what that woman wrote was it? God, Grant, some review in a cheap weekly newspaper is no reason to cry."

Again, Grant nodded. He opened his mouth. No words came out.

"Never mind." Tears dripped from Pauline's eyes. "You're not going to talk again, are you Grant? I know that, have known it, I guess. But that's OK, Grant. It's OK. I love you."

Grant looked into Pauline's eyes. He looked into the damp blackness of the center of his wife's eye, saw there the reflected glow of light from outside as he and Pauline listened to the lingering jazz melodies of Wes Montgomery's guitar, he saw the shimmering illumination of the universe and of eternity reflected in his wife's eye as she sat with him on the floor, clutching her husband's arms, just the two of them in the middle of the suburban night.